C.L.U.T.Z. AND
THE FIZZION FORMULA

C.L.U.T.Z. AND THE FIZZION FORMULA

MARILYN Z. WILKES

pictures by Larry Ross

Dial Books for Young Readers
New York

Published by
Dial Books for Young Readers
A Division of E. P. Dutton
2 Park Avenue
New York, New York 10016

Design by Nancy R. Leo
Printed in the U.S.A.
First edition
COBE
10 9 8 7 6 5 4 3 2 1

Library of Congress Cataloging in Publication Data
Wilkes, Marilyn Z. / C.L.U.T.Z. and the fizzion formula.
Summary / Eleven-year-old Rodney, his guardian robot Clutz,
and his dog Aurora are mistaken as industrial spies
when they wander into a soda factory where a new secret
product named Fizzion is being manufactured.
1. Children's stories, American.
[1. Science fiction. 2. Robots—Fiction.]
I. Ross, Larry, 1943–   ill. II. Title.
III. Title: C.L.U.T.Z. and the fizzion formula.
PZ7.W64839Cam 1985 [Fic] 84-23311
ISBN 0-8037-0171-3 / ISBN 0-8037-0179-9 (lib. bdg.)

For Josh and Ben, again

C.L.U.T.Z. AND
THE FIZZION FORMULA

Rodney Pentax peered out through the bronze glass windows of the leisure room and searched the sky. Beyond the sleek towers of the John Glenn Living Complex he could see the spiral trail of jet rotors and sunlight winking off a tiny windshield.

"The helicab is coming!" he yelled. He raced down the hall of the living unit to his parents' bedroom, dodging the luggage packs lined up outside their door. Aurora Borealis, Rodney's fuzzy pink *Muttus primaverus*, ran after him, barking loudly.

Clutz, the Pentax family's robot, tottered to the

window and watched the approaching jet taxi with an earnest, glassy stare. If only the helicab were coming for him, too. How he would love to be going to Mars with Mr. and Mrs. Pentax. Or even to the spaceport with Rodney to see them off. Being a domestic robot was so confining.

Clutz sighed. He thought of his friends GT–43, an automated jetcar who could span vast highways in a single bound, and often did. Then there was CLUTA–9, that bronze lovely built for deep-space travel. When he had last heard from her, she was on a six-annum research mission to Pluto. Brilliant, beautiful CLUTA–9—Clutz's ROM crystals vibrated just thinking about her. Without a doubt, she was the best of the Combined Level Units/Type A.

But Clutz was not a Type A and knew he could not expect to go dashing around the universe. He was only a Combined Level Unit/Type Z, one of a class introduced for household use some fifty annums earlier.

Only a Type Z; Clutz sighed again. True, Type Z's were pioneers in the field. They were the first robots to have human emotions as well as intellectual and mechanical skills. But as time passed, newer and much more fancy models had appeared, and Clutz had eventually become outmoded. Discarded by his previous owners, he had wound up, finally, on the Pentaxes' doorstep, unwanted and homeless.

He had little cause for complaint though, he thought, rubbing a dent in one arm (the result of a trip down a trash conveyor chute). He wasn't much to look at. His brass-alloy finish was badly oxidized. And there was something cockeyed about the way his joints held together, so that he looked as if he might topple over at any moment. Then there was the small coiled spring that sprouted from one ear. It *boing*ed up and down whenever he moved.

Still, Rodney thought he was the most wonderful robot in the entire galaxy, an opinion for which Clutz was supremely grateful. Where Rodney was concerned, his emotions programming was fully utilized.

Clutz focused on the speck that was the approaching taxi, and his ear spring trembled. "How wonderful to be a human," he mused aloud. "To journey all the way to Mars, to explore unimagined new worlds, to travel around the block without getting lost—"

"Travel isn't so wonderful when you've been

doing it every month for five annums," said Mr. Pentax, coming in with a luggage pack under each arm. "But I suppose it will be a treat for Mrs. Pentax. Lyra, what's *in* these bags, moon rocks?"

"Just the bare essentials, dear," said Mrs. Pentax. "Porta-skis and rocket rackets, running suits, swim suits, exercise suits, evening suits—they dress for dinner at the Space Spa—and a dozen book-films and two viewers."

"We'll only be gone for three weeks," said Mr. Pentax, "and I have to work during the first one."

"It won't take you a week to learn how to be a regional manager," said Lyra Pentax. "You've been Asteroid Candy Company's best salesman in the Earth-to-Mars territory for four annums—"

"Five," said Arthur Pentax.

"Five annums," said his wife. "And it isn't often I get three whole weeks away from F.O.R.K. I intended to make the most of them." Mrs. Pentax was a subregional coordinating supervisor at the Food on Request Korp.

"I sure wish I could go to Mars with you," Rodney said wistfully.

"So do I, son," said his father, putting his arm around Rodney, "but you can't miss school. Besides, this will give you a chance to be with Grandma Deedee and Sandor. You haven't seen them since the wedding."

Rodney was eager to see his grandmother again. She had lived with them from the time he was born until the previous spring, when she had met and quickly married a lively, snowy-haired ex-space pilot named Sandor Grolnik. After the wedding they had moved to a fancy new condominium on Satellite for Seniors, on the Venus Route. Now Grandma and Sandor were coming to stay with Rodney while his parents were away. Their shuttle flight was scheduled to arrive at the spaceport an hour before the Pentaxes' departure.

The doorbell rang.

"There's the taxi," said Lyra Pentax. "Are we ready? Have we forgotten anything?" She bustled around distractedly.

The bell rang again. Aurora trotted over and pressed a button in the doorframe with her large black nose. The door slid open to reveal a chubby, moon-faced man in a shiny, baby-blue jumpsuit with little white wings sticking out above his shoulder blades.

"Arty's Angels Helijet Taxi Service," he announced. " 'We provide a heavenly ride.' Somebody here order a helicab to the spaceport?"

They loaded the luggage into an elevator in the center of the circular hallway and rode up to the roof. There was barely enough room in the small helijet to cram everything in. Mr. and Mrs. Pentax squeezed into the back seat with Rodney between them. Clutz stood watching the luggage packs being loaded, a sorrowful look in his glassy eyes. Rodney's heart melted.

"Can't Clutz come to the spaceport with us?" he begged.

"Mustn't overload the cab," warned the pilot.

"He doesn't weigh much," Rodney persisted. "Please? If Clutz comes, I won't feel so bad that you're going to Mars and leaving me at home." He sighed his most pitiful sigh.

Mr. and Mrs. Pentax looked at each other. Rodney grinned and motioned to Clutz.

"Oh, thank you," said the robot excitedly. He hurried into the front seat and clambered on top of a luggage pack. "I've never been to a spaceport before."

Aurora barked indignantly and leaped into the back seat, where she sprawled on Rodney's lap and refused to budge. If everyone else was going to the spaceport, you can bet they weren't going to leave *her* behind.

"Anyone else you want to bring?" growled the pilot. "Next-door neighbors? Space Scout troop? Moonball team?" He straightened his little white wings and revved up the helijet engines. "I hope this crate makes it," he muttered.

The helijet engines hummed. Its jet rotors whirred, and in a moment they were airborne, whizzing unevenly toward the spaceport at the edge of Sector 5.

As they bounced along over ParkSec, the little helijet suddenly faltered and lost altitude. "Rodney!" cried Clutz in terror. "We're falling out of the sky!"

"Don't be scared," Rodney tried to reassure him. "It's just air currents."

"It's overloading," grumbled the pilot. He pulled on the control stick, and the machine lurched upward.

"Oooooh," squealed Clutz, toppling off his perch on the luggage packs. He grabbed frantically for something to hold on to and found the control stick. The helijet plummeted. Rodney's heart

leaped into his throat as they shaved the tops off a stand of trees and made a direct run at a holovision tower.

"Let go, Clutz!" he yelled.

Swearing like a space pirate, the helijet pilot yanked Clutz loose from the control stick, fired his auxiliaries, and climbed a few meters higher. Everyone heaved a sigh of relief.

"I'm very sorry," Clutz apologized. "I think I'm allergic to heights."

Fifteen minutes later everyone, except Clutz, could finally see the gleaming silver domes of the Arthur C. Clarke Spaceport in the distance. Clutz couldn't see anything because he had hidden his face between his knees and wouldn't open his eyes.

The spaceport was a vast and busy place, one of the largest in the whole United Federation of North America. It had been built as a shuttleport for flights from the Northeast Sector to U.F.N.A.'s local space satellites, including those from which long-distance flights were launched. Recently, however, some of the shorter interplanetary flights, such as the one the Pentaxes were about to take, were being launched directly from Earth. Rodney was glad he had worn his minicam wrist camera.

He was going to take pictures of every spaceship he saw.

The helicab headed for a taxi pad near the glass-domed main terminal. The building looked to Rodney like a huge crystalline spider with curved, tunnel-like legs. Along each leg were launch pads for various kinds of space flights. Travelers reached the launch pads by way of pneumatic train cars that flowed back and forth inside the glass tunnels.

The Pentaxes climbed out of the helicab. Mr. Pentax paid for the ride by inserting his plastoid credit I.D. into a meter slot in the dashboard. He and Mrs. Pentax loaded their luggage packs onto a motorized cart, and they all headed for the check-in area at the entrance to the terminal. There, a stationary robot scanned and stamped the bags and deposited them in a conveyor tube. It also stamped the Pentaxes' tickets and verified their slumber-lounge reservations on B deck, row 23, of their spacecraft.

Inside, the terminal was bustling with activity. Large, thin telecom screens, suspended from the ceiling, blinked with flight information. Electronic voices announced changes in schedules, arrivals and departures, and messages for passengers. Over all were the sounds of people rushing to and from their destinations and the deep, steady roar of spaceships. Rodney loved it. Clutz was dazzled.

"How do we know where to go?" he asked.

Rodney pointed to a telecom screen hanging overhead. "See?" he said. "Fourth line from the top. 'Interplanetary Flight 728 arr. Torus 3/Sat. for Srs.—13:00, Pad 23.' That's Grandma's flight, down that tunnel over there. Pads sixteen to twenty-three."

Mr. Pentax spotted a book-film stall. "Hold on while I pick up a *Daily Newsfilm*," he said.

"I'd like something else to read, too," said Mrs. Pentax. "You three wait right here."

"Sure, Mom," said Rodney.

"Oh, Rodney, look," said Clutz. He trotted over to a luggage check-in chute near the tunnel. "Here are more robots like the one that took your parents' luggage. Primitive fellows, aren't they? Do you suppose they can communicate?" He addressed one of the stationary robots: "Say, there, cousin, bagged any good bags lately?"

The robot blinked a red light, then trained its single scanner eye on him. For a moment Rodney could see a complete map of Clutz's internal circuits displayed on the screen above the luggage chute. Then the robot clamped its right gripper on Clutz's shoulder, stamped *FLT 606* across his breastplate with the other, and pushed him into the pneumatic luggage chute.

"HELP!" cried Clutz, as he was sucked into the mouth of the chute. He held on with both hands, but first one leg and then the other was drawn into the tunnel by the powerful air current. Rodney grabbed his arms and pulled the other way, but he wasn't strong enough.

A crowd gathered around them and tried to help Rodney pull Clutz to safety. One man grabbed him around the middle, but he quickly let go as his jacket whooshed into the chute, along with his instant video camera and *Backpacker's Guide to the Moon*.

"Rodney!" wailed Clutz. "Don't let go. I don't have a round-trip ticket." Rodney tried to hang on, but it looked as if Clutz would be carried into the hold of Flight 606, wherever it was going. "You should be deactivated for this!" he yelped at the red-eyed baggage handler.

Just then an alarm sounded, and a uniformed spaceport supervisor came running toward them. The stationary robot bent over and pressed a large red button next to the mouth of the chute. At once the pneumatic suction stopped, and Clutz tumbled out onto the floor with a crash.

"Something the matter here?" asked the supervisor.

"Not anymore, thank you," said Rodney, with great relief. "The luggage robot shut off the machine." He pulled Clutz to his feet and thanked everyone for their help. The supervisor checked the luggage robot over briefly, then hurried off in search of other problems.

"It—it shut off the machine?" sputtered Clutz. "*Why*, when I was almost *swallowed up*, did it suddenly remember how to shut off the machine?" He straightened his breastplate with such a jerk that he nearly fell down again.

"Maybe its reactions aren't too good," said Rodney. "You said it was a primitive mechanism. Maybe it didn't understand what was happening."

The baggage robot had switched the luggage chute back on and was busily scanning and stamping bags again. Clutz glared at it. The robot paused for a moment, trained its eye on Clutz, and blinked its red light.

"It understood all right, or I am an android's uncle," said Clutz.

Mr. and Mrs. Pentax hurried over. "Where have

you been?" asked Rodney's father. "We turn our backs long enough to buy a newsfilm, and you disappear. Come on, we have to get to the Arrivals area."

"Sorry, Dad," said Rodney. "We were just—uh —inspecting the baggage chute."

"Well, let's go now," said his father. "We don't want to miss Grandma and Sandor."

A small gong sounded and a metallic voice announced, *"Attention, all those awaiting the arrival of Interplanetary flight seven two eight from Torus Colony Three and Satellite for Seniors: There will be a two-hour delay due to meteor-shower activity. Stand by for further information."*

"That's Mother and Sandor's flight!" said Mrs. Pentax. "They're not going to arrive until after we leave. Arthur, we'll have to postpone our departure."

"I can't do that, Lyra," said Mr. Pentax. "I have to be at the Regional Office first thing Wednesday morning. But you can stay over and take a flight out tomorrow if it would make you feel better."

"Oh, come on, Mom," said Rodney. "I'm not a baby—I'm twelve annums old! You don't have to hang around and hold my hand. I'll just wait with Clutz and Aurora until Grandma and Sandor get here. We can watch spaceships. It'll be great."

"I don't know," said Mrs. Pentax. "What if they're delayed further? You could be alone for hours."

"I'm not alone," said Rodney. "Clutz and Aurora are with me."

Clutz put his arm around Rodney's shoulder. "Please do not concern yourself about Master Rodney," he said in his most responsible voice mode. "I will take care of him as I am programmed to do. I won't let him out of my sight for a moment."

Aurora flopped down next to Rodney and rested her chin protectively on his foot.

Mrs. Pentax considered the situation. "I *was* looking forward to a long, leisurely flight with your father. What do you think, Arthur?"

"I think it's a shame to spoil your vacation over a simple delay," said Mr. Pentax. "Rodney will be all right. That's why we have a robot, isn't it—to take care of him?" He gave Clutz a stern look. "But I want you to know that I hold you responsible for my son's welfare. Do your job properly and no slipups, or else."

"Oh, no sir, yes sir," said Clutz. He stepped

backward and tripped over Aurora. "You can count on me, sir."

Another gong sounded, and the metallic voice announced: *"All those departing Clipper Class on Trans-Galaxy flight three four to satellites Alpha and Epsilon and the planet Mars may now proceed to Launch Area Eight for early boarding. This is the first call."*

"That's us," said Mr. Pentax. "We might as well go to our gate."

They stepped into a pneumatic car and rode swiftly down the tunnel to Launch Area 8, where a flight steward checked their tickets and directed them to the preboarding lounge. A young lady in a green jumpsuit with **TG** on the pocket was handing out No-Grav Anti-Nausea Tabs.

"Just peel off the backing and press it behind your ear," she told Rodney's parents. "Then you won't feel sick when we lift off and leave Earth's gravity. Weightlessness doesn't agree with some people," she explained to Rodney.

The second boarding call sounded. "I guess this is it," said Mr. Pentax. Rodney's mother gave him a hug and a kiss.

"You're sure you'll be all right?" she asked.

"Yes, Mom," Rodney assured her.

"And you know where to meet Grandma and Sandor?"

"Quit worrying, Mom," said Rodney.

His father gave him a hug and a handful of Nutri-Sweets and shook the paw that Aurora offered. Then he and Mrs. Pentax walked up the boarding ramp, through the airlock, and into the giant spaceship.

Rodney, Clutz, and Aurora made a dash for the glass-roofed observation dome atop the terminal to watch the liftoff. Looking down, they could see the big spaceship sitting on its pad, engines humming, rows of tiny windows lining its oval sides. The captain and crew were busy in the lighted bubble on top of the craft.

"That must be B deck," said Rodney, pointing to the second row of windows. "I think I see Mom waving." He quickly finished munching on a hand-ful of Nutri-Sweets, then snapped some pictures with his wrist camera.

Suddenly the ship began to vibrate. Its roaring gathered volume; its oval bottom glowed. As the three of them watched, the spacecraft lifted up-ward into the atmosphere, gathering speed. They kept their eyes on it as it shrank to a speck and, in a moment, was out of sight.

· 2 ·

"Well," said Rodney, "they're gone."

"Couldn't we stay awhile longer and watch the spaceships?" asked Clutz. "A domestic robot doesn't often find himself at a spaceport, you know."

"Sure," said Rodney. "I love watching space-ships. Besides, I want to take some more pictures. I've only been here a few times myself. Wow! Look at that silver delta-wing rocket coming in nose first. I'd sure love to pilot one of those someday. Or maybe a jumbo saucer like that blue one." He snapped away happily with his wrist camera.

"That would be thrilling, Rodney," said Clutz. "Just like Captain Stalwart." Captain Stalwart was the hero of Clutz's favorite holovision program, *Galactic Spy*. He tried never to miss it.

"Captain Stalwart can pilot any spacecraft ever built," confided Clutz. "He said so in 'Captain Stalwart Fights the Gworkon Menace.' Remember how he and his trusty navigator Cosmo out-maneuvered the Gworkons in that solar rocket? Perhaps I could be your trusty navigator. All I would need is a bit of astral programming."

Rodney laughed. "You and your Captain Stalwart. Sometimes I think you believe he really exists."

"He does, to me," said Clutz.

They watched the big blue saucer settle onto its landing pad. "That round spaceship makes me think of protoburgers," said Rodney. "It must be almost lunchtime. You two stay here while I go get something to eat. Hungry, Aurora?"

Aurora barked and got up to follow Rodney. She wasn't going to let him wander around a strange spaceport all by himself. She gave Clutz a nudge.

"I think I had better come, too," said the robot.

"I did promise your father I would take good care of you."

There was a Robo-Snak unit on the main level near Tunnel 3. Rodney looked over the rows of colored pictures of the foods dispensed by the machine.

"Please make your selection," said the Robo-Snak. Rodney took out his credit I.D. and inserted it in the slot.

"Two protoburgers and a GalactiCola, please," he said. A window slid open near the bottom of the machine. Out came two steaming burgers and a frosty cylinder of GalactiCola on a disposa-tray.

"Bon appétit," said the Robo-Snak.

"Thank you," said Rodney. He picked up the tray of food and looked for a comfortable place to sit.

"Perhaps we should go to Area Twenty-three and await your grandparents," said Clutz. "There might be a place for you to sit down and eat there." Rodney handed a protoburger to Aurora and nodded.

They hopped a pneumatic train to Area 23 and found seats in the lounge. Rodney pulled the silver tab off the nozzle on the GalactiCola container and took a swallow. GalactiCola was his favorite soft drink—Aurora's, too. He poured some into the disposa-tray for her. She lapped at it daintily.

As they munched on their burgers, other people began to drift in. A young couple carrying a baby girl sat down opposite them. The baby was dressed in a fuzzy pink jumpsuit. The wisp of hair on top of her head was tied with a big pink ribbon. Aurora saw the fuzzy pink bundle, and immediately love filled her heart. She whined and wagged her tail so hard that Rodney thought she would sprain it.

When the baby saw Aurora, she laughed and waved her arms with delight. Aurora trotted over and laid her head in the infant's lap, nuzzling and making little woofing noises. The baby giggled louder and pulled Aurora's floppy ears. Her mother was alarmed by the intrusion. "*Shoo, doggy*," she said. "Go away."

Rodney hurried over. "Don't worry. Aurora's just crazy about babies," he explained. "Especially babies in fuzzy pink suits. It brings out her maternal instincts or something. Come on, Aurora, that's enough."

Aurora gave the baby a last adoring nuzzle and reluctantly followed Rodney across the room. The baby set up a howl of disappointment. Aurora whined sympathetically.

The soft gong sounded again, and the familiar electronic voice came over the loudspeaker: *"Attention, please. Interplanetary flight seven two eight from Torus Colony Three and Satellite for Seniors has experienced further delay owing to meteor damage to the spacecraft. Repairs are taking place in flight. Estimated time of arrival is now Monday, fifteen hundred hours."* The gong sounded once more.

There was a flurry of noise and activity in the lounge as the meaning of this latest announcement sank in.

"Great galaxies!" Rodney exploded. "They won't be here until *tomorrow*! What are we supposed to do now?"

"Go back to the observation dome and watch more spaceships?" offered Clutz hopefully.

"Until tomorrow afternoon? We can't stay here all day and all night," said Rodney. His mother had been right. She never should have left him. He wished she were here now.

"It will be all right," Clutz reassured him. "You

and Aurora can sleep right here in the lounge, and I'll watch over you as I promised your parents I would. We'll take care of each other."

Rodney thought about it. Maybe it would be all right. He wasn't a baby, after all, and he did have Clutz and Aurora.

"I guess nobody would mind," he said. "We could have protoburgers and GalactiCola for dinner and breakfast, too." He was beginning to like the idea more and more.

Clutz nodded. "It will be an adventure," he said. "Just like Captain Stalwart."

Rodney laughed. "It's a good thing I have my credit I.D.," he said. "My credit I.D.! Oh no!" He felt in all his jumpsuit pockets. "I left it in the Robo-Snak!" He jumped up and tore out of the lounge. Clutz and Aurora ran after him.

They found him at the Robo-Snak stand, peering into its compartments and examining the floor around it. *"Please make your selection,"* the machine kept saying over and over.

"It's no use," said Rodney. "My credit I.D. is gone. Somebody must have taken it."

"Mugged!" cried Clutz. "We've been mugged! Robbed! Burgled! And we've been here only an hour! How could I have let this happen? Mr. and

Mrs. Pentax will be furious. They'll probably have me recycled, and I deserve it! I was supposed to take care of you. Oh dear, Rodney, what will we do? What will we do?" Clutz slumped against the Robo-Snak for support.

"Please make your selection," said the Robo-Snak.

"I guess we'd better report it to the authorities," said Rodney. He patted Clutz on the shoulder and took his arm.

They found a Travelers' Information Center near the check-in area. A young woman whose badge said COURTESY PERSON listened sympathetically. Then she asked Rodney to sign his name and I.D. number on a computer pad and explain into its recorder exactly what had happened.

"Don't worry," she said when he was finished. "This cancels your old card immediately. A new one will be in your home mail chute first thing tomorrow morning."

Rodney thanked her.

"See?" said Clutz, patting Rodney on the shoulder and taking his arm. "I knew everything would be all right. What a nice human person! What efficiency! You'll have a new card tomorrow morning."

"Yes, but that won't help us today," said Rodney. "I won't be able to buy food for Aurora and me. We can't stay here all day and all night without eating. I should have saved those Nutri-Sweets. Now we'll have to go home and come back tomorrow."

Clutz was again dejected. "How inconvenient that living things must consume nourishment!" he said. "Robots are fortunate in that respect. A fresh battery pack, and we're good for annums." He brightened a bit. "Well, then, suppose we go back to the observation dome and watch the spaceships for a while before we take the helicab home? We might as well enjoy ourselves, as long as we're here."

"We can't take a helicab home," said Rodney. "I can't pay for it. No credit I.D., remember? We'll have to take the moving walkways. Sometimes I wish we still used money, the way they did in the old days. Not as convenient as a credit I.D., maybe, but—"

"Take the moving walkways! All the way to Sector Three?" Clutz was truly dismayed. "But it's so far, and we don't know the way. We'll get lost, I know we will. I always get lost. It's one of the things I do best."

"We'll be okay," said Rodney, trying to reassure them both. "We'll just follow the signs. We'd better get going, though, because it could take a long time."

Clutz cast a wistful farewell glance at the observation dome, then followed Rodney and Aurora toward the glass exit doors of the spaceport.

"Don't worry. You'll be back tomorrow," said Rodney.

"It's a long time until tomorrow," said Clutz.

·꒳·

Outside the spaceport there was total confusion.
The pavement was jammed with pedestrians and
motorized baggage carts. Helicabs whizzed in and
out overhead, dropping off and picking up passengers. Every minute or so a spaceship landed or
departed with a roar. Rodney, Clutz, and Aurora
stared bewildered, trying to decide which way to
go.

"Over there," said Rodney, pointing to a distant
ramp. "That sign says 'To Central Sector.' I'm
sure we can find our way to Sector Three once we
get that far. Come on."

It wasn't as easy as Rodney had expected. The walkways were crowded and confusing. Exit ramps and overpasses sprouted everywhere. People elbowed from one side to the other, pushing the three of them off balance. Rodney clung to Aurora with one hand and to Clutz with the other as they sped along.

"I don't see any signs to Central Sector," said Clutz. "If I'm not mistaken, we must have gone too far."

"I don't think so," said Rodney. He craned his head to see the next sign. "Look, over there. It says 'Central Sector Bypass/Sectors Three–Four, Alternate Route.' That must be a shortcut. Let's take it."

"We'd better not, Rodney," said Clutz. "We'll get lost. I can feel it in my circuits."

Aurora barked loudly. She felt lost already. She wasn't a bloodhound, after all.

"Stop worrying. We'll be okay as long as we can read the signs," said Rodney. "Come on. This could save us a lot of time."

They zigzagged across the walkway to the outer lane, dodging a large lady in a purple cape and her three purple-clad children. They got off onto the exit ramp and circled around under the main walkway, onto a smaller one. Now there was almost no traffic.

"Whew! I sure am glad to get away from those crowds," said Rodney.

"But where are we?" asked Clutz anxiously. He was still a little dizzy from the walkways. "This doesn't look like Sector Three. We're lost, aren't we? I knew we would be."

"Will you stop talking about getting lost?" said Rodney. "We're just not there yet."

They were passing through an area of light industry. Sprawling factory buildings and warehouses dotted the landscape. Holographic signs advertised *CompuToys Unlimited, Bio-Snak Industries,* and *Jetaway Jumpsuits—For a Far-Out Fit!* There were no people or helijets anywhere in sight.

"It's so deserted," said Clutz. "Rodney, why is it so deserted? Where is everyone?"

"Sunday isn't one of the four workdays," said Rodney. "You know that. Besides, all these factories are roboticized. It only takes a couple of humans to supervise a whole plant. I learned all about it in Technology class."

"Why don't we find one of those human supervisors and ask directions to Sector Three?" asked Clutz. "I would utilize my directional circuits, but they haven't worked properly in over twenty annums."

Rodney grinned. "Some trusty navigator *you'd* make," he said. "Oh, okay. We'll stop and ask for directions."

They exited at the next ramp and walked down a deserted street to the nearest building. It was large and gray and octagonal, with narrow window slits all around the top. On the roof was a glowing red-and-blue sign:

○○○○○○○○○○○○○○○○○○○○○○
○　　　　　　　　　　　　　　　　　　　○
○　　**GALACTICOLA**　　○
○　　　(Div. U.F.N.A. Foods)　　　○
○　Blending & Filling Plant No. 3　○
○○○○○○○○○○○○○○○○○○○○○○

"Wow, this is where they make GalactiCola!" said Rodney, running toward the building and snapping a couple of pictures. "I can't believe it! That's Aurora and my favorite drink, right, girl? Maybe we can get some free samples while we're— Oof!"

He collided head-on with a little old man in a glittering mirrored jumpsuit.

"Excuse me," said Rodney. "I'm really sorry. I didn't see you."

"Didn't see you myself—quite all right," said the little man, tucking a shock of white hair back into the shiny hood of his suit. "Forget it, please!" He scurried off toward the plant in a flash of sparkling light and disappeared around a corner.

"Hey!" yelled Rodney. "Wait a minute! Do you know how to get to Sector Three?"

"He didn't seem eager to chat," said Clutz.

"Then we'll have to ask somebody else," said Rodney, starting off in the same direction the old man had gone. He took two steps forward, when the air in front of him suddenly crackled with thin streams of burning white light. He leaped back in a hurry.

"A laser fence!" he said. "Now, why would they have a laser fence around a soda factory? And why didn't it stop that guy in the fancy suit?"

"I don't know, and I don't think I care to find out," exclaimed Clutz, tottering back toward the street. "If they want their privacy, it's quite all right with me. We can ask for directions somewhere else. I'd rather not sizzle my circuits, if you don't mind."

"Wait a minute," called Rodney, running after him. "This is a great opportunity. We can't pass it up. Don't you want to see the inside of a real soda factory, full of robots just like you? It might be really interesting. And I'd love another Galacti-Cola. I split the last one with Aurora. Come on! The worst that can happen is that they'll just tell us to go away."

"The worst that can happen is that we'll be melted like lava by that nasty invisible laser," said Clutz.

"It's just a security system to keep out trespassers," said Rodney. "We're not trespassers. We're travelers who need directions and a cold drink. That's not too much to ask, is it?"

"They must think so, or they wouldn't have put that overgrown insta-broiler between our ask and their answer," replied Clutz.

Rodney laughed. He picked up a pebble and tossed it a few feet in front of him. It disintegrated in a puff of smoke.

"I rest my case," said Clutz.

Aurora began sniffing back and forth along the

ground. She crouched as low as she could and crept forward a foot or two, then carefully raised her head a few inches. The white light flashed, and the pink bow on top of her head sizzled sharply. She yelped, ducked, and moved forward a few more feet, keeping her body as close to the ground as she possibly could. Finally she raised her head again, then slowly stood up and began racing around in circles.

"Aurora got under the fence!" exclaimed Rodney. "The lasers don't reach all the way to the ground! Good girl, Aurora! Come on, Clutz—if Aurora can do it, so can we."

"Really, Rodney," said Clutz, "I don't think this is a good idea. Your father would never—"

But Rodney had already dropped to his stomach and was worming his way toward Aurora. Trembling with apprehension, Clutz clattered to the ground and followed him.

"Keep your rear end down," cautioned Rodney as a laser seared Clutz's posterior.

"How fortunate that my intelligence modules are located elsewhere," said Clutz, rubbing the melted spot on his backside. "At least I think they are.

"Now what do you propose?" asked the robot

apprehensively as they stood up and brushed themselves off. "I don't see an entrance anywhere. It still isn't too late to leave before—"

A door opened in one side of the building, and a row of large, grim-looking sentry robots filed out and rolled toward them.

"Rodney, look!" exclaimed Clutz. "An unwelcoming committee! I knew it! We're going to be attacked!"

"Don't be silly," said Rodney. "They're just robot guards. Now maybe we'll get what we came for. Hey, you guys . . ." He waved to the roguards. "Can you help us? We need directions, and a cold drink."

The row of sentries rolled up and surrounded them. "You–will–come–with–us," they said in unison.

A growl rumbled in Aurora's throat. She moved closer to Rodney.

The three were taken around to the side of the building. One of the roguards pressed a button, and a narrow door slid open. Behind it stood a thin, olive-skinned man with frazzled red hair wearing a scientist's white lab coat.

"So!" exclaimed the man. "They've tried again, this time with a child, a dog, and a ridiculous ruin of a robot. Will they stop at nothing? Do they think we're fools?"

"Sir?" said Rodney timidly. "We're sorry to bother you, but we'd like directions to Sector Three, if you don't mind."

"Is that why you sneak under the fence like thieves?" demanded the man. "Bring them inside," he snapped at the roguards.

· 4 ·

"On my honor as a Space Scout," insisted Rodney as they were pushed toward the door of the factory, "we're just trying to find our way home from the spaceport. We took the wrong exit, that's all. Nobody sent us."

"We shall see," growled the man. "Your I.D. card, please."

"I don't have my I.D. card with me, but my name is Rodney Pentax, and this is my dog Aurora, and this is my robot Clutz." He put a protective arm around each of them. "We're from Sector Three, the John Glenn Living Complex, and we were coming back from the spaceport, like I said. My parents just left on a trip to Mars, but my grandma and her new husband didn't get here in time to meet us, so we have to go home and—"

"Enough!" cried the man, holding up his hand. "You say you have no I.D. card. That is most unusual. We will have to verify your identity. See to it," he said to one of the roguards. It rolled away into the bowels of the building. Clutz whispered something into Rodney's ear.

"No secrets!" barked the little man. "I hate secrets! Unless, of course, they're my secrets." He smiled a nasty smile. "I have jim-dandy secrets. But they're for me to know and for you not to find out!" He scowled. "Now, what did the robot say? *Tell me!*"

Clutz jumped and scurried behind Rodney.

"He said that human factory workers have a peculiar way of greeting visitors," answered Rodney, standing up straighter. He was trying to be brave. Behind him Clutz did the same. "And he thinks you should tell us your name, since we told you ours." Clutz peeked out from behind Rodney, nodded, and waved shyly.

The red-haired scientist eyed Clutz with hostility. "Of course, how rude. Forgive me. I always introduce myself to intruders. I am Dr. Greps. Dr. Seymor Greps," he said, bowing slightly.

Clutz bowed back, banging Rodney on top of the head with his forehead.

"However, I am not a factory worker," said the scientist. "Here we have robots for that purpose. I am Assistant Director of Research and Development for the New Products Division of Galacti-Cola, a division of U.F.N.A. Foods." His voice grew colder.

"But you already know that, don't you? You also know that I have come to Plant Number Three to supervise the production of my newest, most brilliant soft drink, Fizzion." His eyes blazed with pride and anger.

"You know that because you are industrial spies, cleverly disguised as a boy, a dog, and a robot. Why don't you admit it and save us a lot of time? You have been sent here by Planetary Products, our chief rival, to steal my formula and sabotage its production." He began pacing back and forth, gesturing wildly with both hands. "This is not the first attempt by your employers to breach our security. But they have not been successful so far, and they will not be!" He stopped pacing. He was breathing heavily.

"But sir," Rodney protested. "We aren't disguised as a boy, a dog, and a robot. We *are* a boy, a dog, and a robot—anybody can see that. We're not spies. I'm not even old enough to have a job."

"No? Then why aren't you carrying an I.D.?" Dr. Greps grabbed Rodney's forearm. "And why do you wear this wrist camera, if not to photograph secrets?"

"So I could take pictures of the rockets at the spaceport," said Rodney. "I'm going to be a pilot someday."

Dr. Greps was unconvinced. "Well, then perhaps you and the dog are simply an unwitting cover," he said, releasing Rodney's arm. "What better disguise than a boy and his faithful *Muttus*?" Aurora gazed adoringly at Rodney and licked his hand. "You could be unaware of the real purpose of your intrusion.

"But the robot . . ." The scientist jabbed Clutz with his index finger. "That is another matter."

"Careful, please," said Clutz. "I dent easily."

Dr. Greps glowered at him. "Perhaps," said the scientist, "this robot has brought you here to carry out industrial espionage for which it was programmed weeks or even months ago. Many secret devices can be built into a robot—even one so disreputable-looking as this. A clever touch, the disreputableness. Such an antique doesn't look capable of anything. However, it will be examined for concealed cameras, computer erasure units, explosives—"

"Explosives?" Clutz was horrified. "You mean as in 'to blow oneself up'? Oh no—I assure you, I like all my parts in their present arrangement, antique or not. I couldn't do any of the things you suggest. I am programmed to be totally honest and upright. I cannot tell a lie, not even a fib."

"That's true," said Rodney. "He can't."

"We'll soon see," said Dr. Greps grimly. "I will take you to Dr. Rench. *She* will discover the truth." Rodney, Clutz, and Aurora shivered. "Follow me," ordered the scientist.

The roguards surrounded them and ushered them into the factory.

As they stepped through the doorway, Rodney gasped. Although he had learned a few things about roboticized factories from his History of Technology class, he had never visited one. The GalactiCola plant was more fantastic than anything he had read about or imagined. The huge eight-sided building hummed with bizarre activity. Each section was packed with groups of weird-

looking robots working at different tasks. There were big box-shaped robots twice his height, with forklift arms and wheels instead of feet, unloading rolls of packaging material. Squat multi-armed robots slithered back and forth like crabs, feeding long strips of the stiff paper into gas-filled sterilizing units. When the paper emerged, it had been formed into long, skinny tubes. These were nipped off into small cylinders and carried by conveyor belts to stationary, armless robots with fat, round bodies and long, flexible necks.

These strangest of all robots each had a small head at the ends of their necks and a single camera-like "eye." Below each eye were several flexible "fingers" or a hoselike "mouth." The robots filled or sealed or labeled the cylinders, bending and swaying with eerie grace in a programmed series of motions. It looked like a vast, weird ballet. Rodney almost thought he heard music.

"Rodney," said Clutz anxiously, "these creatures don't look very friendly. You said they would look like me, but they look like—like monsters!" He held Rodney's arm more tightly.

"I guess they don't have to look humanoid for this kind of work," said Rodney. *"Watch out!"*

A pair of forklift robots careened toward them at high speed, their heavy loads suspended overhead. Dr. Greps screamed. Clutz screamed. The robots veered away just inches from the group and crashed into a conveyor belt. Machine parts and empty Fizzion containers showered the area.

"I think I'd like to go now," said Clutz, trembling.

"Go?" shrieked Dr. Greps. "After almost killing me? We've been having accidents like this all week, and now I know why! You've just exposed your hand, robot! You've blown your cover!"

"But I didn't," insisted Clutz. "Really, I couldn't—"

They were rushed past the area where the soft-drink formula was being prepared. A giant vat gurgled and sloshed as it received the right amount of each ingredient from a maze of overhead pipes. On the front of the vat were dials and flashing lights and a fat glass tube in which a luminous green liquid bubbled. A string of roguards surrounded the area.

"That poisonous-looking substance must be Fizzion," whispered Clutz, still holding Rodney's arm. "It amazes me what humans are willing to put into their bodies." Dr. Greps shot him a dark look. The line of roguards drew together protectively, their robot eyes fastened on Clutz. He hurried past.

They reached the building core, a round glass tower two stories high. A glass elevator took them to a balcony surrounding the tower's second floor. The elevator opened in front of a glass door. A small sign on it said DR. RENATA RENCH, DIRECTOR OF OPERATIONS. Dr. Greps knocked.

"Come in," commanded a woman's voice. The door slid open, revealing a large white room surrounded by windows. Seated on a stool behind a white desk console was a tall, severe-looking woman in a high-necked white jumpsuit and white lab coat. Her flame-red hair was fastened in a knot at the back of her head. She had been watching their approach on a bank of video screens built into the desktop. She punched a row of buttons, and the screens went dark.

"Why have you brought them here?" she asked Dr. Greps. "We have no time to waste on guided tours."

"But Dr. Rench," said Dr. Greps, "they are spies. They claim to be a boy, a robot, and a dog, but—"

"You idiot," snapped Dr. Rench. "They *are* a

boy, a robot, and a dog. The roguard data has been verified. Besides, the boy is too young to have a job. Now, get rid of them. We have work to do."

"But they were trespassing. The boy has a wrist camera, but no identification. And there was an accident. It is all very suspicious." He eyed his captives furtively. They squirmed with discomfort. Renata Rench glared at her associate. "That wasn't the first accident in recent days, as you well know. You also know, better than anyone else, how fatal another interruption in the Fizzion-making process could be. It must be avoided at all costs!"

Her voice grew intense. "Tomorrow," she said, "we launch Fizzion across the far reaches of the planet and beyond, to be drunk by millions upon millions of humans. Must I remind you what that means to both of us? Nothing can be allowed to stand in the way of our success, including these ridiculous delays. Now, get rid of them!" She turned her back and walked to the window to survey a group of robots below.

Dr. Greps sighed like a punctured balloon and motioned to the roguards. Rodney, Clutz, and Aurora were ushered back through the door and into the elevator.

"But we still need directions to Sector Three,"

Rodney cried over his shoulder. The elevator doors closed behind them, and before he knew it they were again outside the laser fence.

Rodney watched the retreating roguards with bewilderment. "What a weird place," he said. "Imagine that guy thinking we were spies." Aurora barked indignantly.

Clutz nervously jiggled his ear spring up and down. "Perhaps the red-haired human had his reasons," he said.

"What do you mean?" asked Rodney.

"That Dr. Greps thought we were spies," said Clutz. "Was that logical? Was it rational? Why was he so suspicious? What could possibly be so special about a new beverage? The universe is full of them.

"But what if that evil-looking green substance is more than just a soft drink?" Clutz stopped jiggling. "Rodney, what if something is going on in that factory, something so secret and terrible that they must protect it with roguards and laser fences to keep anyone from finding out about it? Why else would they have treated us the way they did? It simply doesn't compute, unless . . ."

Clutz lowered his voice and glanced around to

make sure no one could hear them. "Dr. Rench said Fizzion would be sent 'to the far reaches of the planet and beyond, to be drunk by millions upon millions of humans.'

"Rodney, suppose someone, or a group of some-ones, wished to gain control of a planet," he said. "They wouldn't do it by armed force. That would be too messy and destructive; the planet wouldn't be worth having when they were through. But suppose they could gain control over an entire population by persuading everyone to taste a delectable new soft drink. Chemical hypnosis! A few sips would be enough. A whole world could be theirs!"

Rodney put his arm around Clutz. "Now I *know* you've been watching too many Captain Stalwart shows," he said. "I even remember that one. There was this bunch of giant aphids from a planet in Alpha Centauri. They hypnotized everybody through their holovision sets and then put them in cages so they could suck their blood when ever they got hungry. It was disgusting."

"I am not talking about giant aphids, Rodney," insisted Clutz. "That was science fiction. This is reality. I believe I know the difference between the two. But what about Martian Freedom Fighters? Red hair is extremely common on Mars, isn't it?"

"Come on, Clutz," said Rodney. "Martians are just like people from Earth. They *are* people from Earth—originally, I mean."

"Well, all right, perhaps Dr. Greps and Dr. Rench are not Martian Freedom Fighters," said Clutz. "Perhaps they are aliens *disguised* as Martian Freedom Fighters. That would be even worse! And who was that mysterious silver-suited creature we saw on the way in? He could be part of the plot. Don't you see, the humans of this planet may be in grave danger, and we are quite possibly the only ones who know it. We must discover the truth. It is our duty.

"A robot's first duty is to help humans," said Clutz, taking Rodney's hand. "It is in our programming. I must protect you from peril. Besides, I promised your father."

He squared his shoulders with a loud creak. "I have reached a decision," he said. "I am going back into the factory to appropriate a sample of Fizzion, for your sake and for all humankind. It gives me a case of hives just to think about it, but it must be done. When I return, we will go to the

Planetary Police and ask them to have the potion analyzed. If it is only a soft drink, well and good. But if it is more—"

Aurora started to whine.

"Don't try to dissuade me," said Clutz. "I am determined to go back, for Rodney and for humans everywhere." With that, he dropped to his stomach and clanked his way under the laser fence.

"I know you think this is for my own good," said Rodney, "so you're going to do it even if I tell you not to. But I want you to know I don't like it. I don't like it one bit! You could get into big trouble, no matter how things turn out." He watched Clutz for a minute and then sighed. "Come on, Aurora. We've got to go, too. He'll never be able to handle it by himself."

"No, no, stay there! It's too dangerous," insisted Clutz.

"The only way to stop me is not to go yourself," said Rodney, wriggling under the fence. He had made up his mind.

Aurora followed reluctantly. She didn't want to go back into that scary place full of mean-looking machines; but wherever Rodney went, she would follow.

They sneaked around the building and hid

behind a clump of bushes, trying not to alert the roguards. Tiptoeing up to a loading dock in the back, they saw forklift robots hoisting cases of bright-green Fizzion cylinders into giant freight-vans.

"I hope we're not too late," whispered Clutz.

"Why don't we just grab a container and run?" Rodney whispered.

"The cases are sealed," replied Clutz. "Besides, the roguards would catch us before we could reach the fence. We must do this discreetly if we are to be successful." He looked both ways, then flattened himself against the building and awkwardly inched his way inside. Rodney and Aurora followed.

The plant was operating at full tilt. Forklift robots zoomed back and forth, loading and unloading their bright-green cargo. Long-necked stationary robots bobbed and swayed. Conveyor belts lurched past filling and labeling stations. Roguards stood grimly at their posts. And in the center of the factory, overlooking everything, Dr. Greps and Dr. Rench kept watch from their glass-walled tower.

The three scurried along the wall and hid behind a giant tank labeled H_2O. "Do you see that?" whispered Clutz. "That must be part of the secret formula."

Rodney giggled nervously. "It's water, silly," he whispered. "H_2O is the chemical name for water, because it's made of two atoms of hydrogen and one atom of oxygen."

"Aha!" said Clutz. "Then why don't they call it water, if that's what it is, instead of being so mysterious about it? They're hiding something, that's why!"

"Sshhh," whispered Rodney. "They'll hear you."

"EEEE-OOOO-EEEE-OOOO—" Suddenly sirens wailed and lights began flashing all over the plant.

"They've seen us!" Rodney gasped. He was frightened now. Getting caught by two possibly mad scientists after the three of them had already been thrown out of the place was enough to frighten anybody. He knew they shouldn't have come back. Aurora shielded his body with hers and bared her teeth.

"No they haven't," said Clutz, pointing. "Look!"

Every robot had begun doing a frantic dance, going through its paces two or three times faster than normal. Rolls of packaging material fell off racks and unwound across the floor. Conveyor belts raced along lickety-split, while rivers of green cylinders were becoming a flood.

The stationary robots increased their speed in an effort to keep up with the flow, but it was too much for them. Cylinders smashed and splashed to the floor; labels whirled and swirled through the air. The robots twisted and bobbed, spurting glue and squirting soda like demented geese.

"What's gotten into them?" breathed Rodney.

"I don't know, but this is our opportunity," said Clutz. "No one will notice us in all the confusion." He scuttled out from behind a tank, sliding his way toward a speeding conveyor belt.

Rodney's heart was pounding. "Be careful," he whispered. "Don't let them see you."

At the first sound of the alarm, Dr. Rench and Dr. Greps had run out of the glass-walled office onto the balcony overlooking the plant floor. They hurried down in the elevator, arguing heatedly. As they burst out of the elevator, Dr. Rench called out, "GIGO deactivate!"

As if by magic, all motion ceased. The conveyor belts lurched to a stop, spilling their cylinders over the sides with a final splash. Filling robots were suspended in motion, liquid dribbling messily from their spouts. Forklift robots froze where they stood, their loads stuck in midair.

Caught by surprise in the middle of the floor, Clutz looked frantically for a hiding place. He tried to duck into a niche between two storage bins, but the spot was already occupied by a familiar small figure in a glittering jumpsuit. Startled, Clutz backed away, slipped on the wet, paper-strewn tile, and fell with a crash.

"What was that?" asked Dr. Rench.

"The trespassers have returned," shouted Dr. Greps. "Over there!"

"Roguards!" commanded Dr. Rench. "Get them!"

"Let's get out of here!" yelled Rodney.

Clutz struggled to his feet, but it was too late. He and Rodney and Aurora were surrounded by roguards and carried through the plant to the waiting scientists.

"Don't tell them anything," cried Clutz. "And don't drink any Fizzion, no matter what!"

· 5 ·

"But they must be spies," insisted Dr. Greps, scowling at the trembling trio. "Why else would they have returned? And why would another disruption have occurred precisely at that moment?"

"Why, indeed?" asked Dr. Rench, frowning. "Just look at this mess!"

"Now we'll be delayed even further," moaned Dr. Greps. "If the Fizzion isn't sealed and pressurized within four hours after the ingredients are combined, it will be ruined, and so will we. Let me contact Headquarters and tell them we have a problem," he begged. "They could send us additional robots right away, a type that can be individually controlled—"

"No!" snapped Dr. Rench, her violet eyes blazing. "This plant is my responsibility, as the formula is yours. I can solve its problems myself! Headquarters expects it. To ask for help would be to admit that I'm not competent to carry out the assignment. Four hours should be plenty of time."

"But we have to do something," argued Dr. Greps. "If the formula breaks down, valuable ingredients will be wasted. We won't be able to fulfill our orders. Headquarters doesn't look kindly on failure."

"We will not fail," said Dr. Rench grimly. "We will simply work harder to prevent more sabotage. Perhaps these intruders *are* responsible. The evidence certainly points in their direction. But as you say, we can't afford to waste time now. We'll have to interrogate them after we're back on line. Meanwhile, we can't just turn them loose. Take them to storeroom B," she ordered the roguards. "That should keep them out of mischief for a little while."

Their apprehension growing, Rodney, Clutz, and Aurora were ushered into the glass elevator and taken to the basement. They were marched along a brightly lit, tiled corridor until they came to a gray metal door with a letter B on it. The door slid open on a small, dark, windowless room. The roguards pushed the three inside and rolled out, letting the door slide shut behind them.

"Rodney, it's so dark in here," whimpered Clutz. His ear spring was trembling; so was the rest of him. "Did I ever mention that I'm allergic to the dark? Oh, I don't mean the kind of dark that's in your room at night. Just the kind in closets and trash conveyor chutes and basement storerooms. Oh dear, this is all my fault. How will we ever escape from this awful place?"

"If only I had my Space Scout lithium light cell," said Rodney, "we could search for a way out."

"Lithium lights!" exclaimed Clutz. "I forgot all about them! Would you prefer brights or dims?" He blinked twice, and two beams of light shone from his eye sockets; one more blink and the light softened. "There," he sighed, "that's better. I haven't used these in annums. It's a good thing lithium batteries don't wear out. They're the only parts I have left that are still under warranty."

They were in what appeared to be a storeroom for spare machine parts. Odd chunks of robot bodies poked out of boxes and lay propped against the walls. Rodney felt as if one might jump out and grab him. Swallowing his fear, he searched the room until he found a long metal bar from a gripper arm.

"Help me with this, Clutz," he said. Together they wedged the bar between the storeroom door and the doorframe and pushed. The door slid open a few inches.

"When I get this open far enough," he whispered, "make a rocket-line for the nearest exit."

"But we mustn't forget our mission," insisted Clutz. "We still must get what we came for."

"I thought you were scared," said Rodney. "I thought you wanted to get out of here."

"I am; I do," said Clutz, "but a robot has to do what a robot has to do."

They pushed open the storeroom door and peered out. Clutz saw a brief flash, like light reflected off a mirror.

"What was that?" he asked Rodney.

"What was what?" asked Rodney.

Clutz looked again, but the hallway was empty.

Leaving the metal bar wedged in the doorframe just in case, they tiptoed off in search of a stairway or a passage to the outside. The elevator, they decided, was too risky.

They passed several doors along the corridor, but all of them were locked. Then they saw one marked

> # CAUTION
> ## CRYOGENIC CHAMBER
> ## AUTHORIZED PERSONNEL ONLY

"What do you suppose is in there?" asked Clutz.

"Well, we know that *cryogenic* means supercold," reasoned Rodney. "It could be a big cryobin, like the one we keep food in at home."

"You mean a cold-storage room for GalactiCola products?" said Clutz. "If so, we could collect a sample of Fizzion."

"As long as we do it fast," said Rodney nervously. "I don't like all this spy stuff. I just want to go home." He glanced up and down the hall, took a deep breath, and pushed a button on the wall. The door slid open.

It was a medium-sized room, well lit, and lined with panels of lustrous gray metal.

"I don't think this is a cryobin," whispered Rodney.

"It certainly isn't a storeroom," said Clutz.

The room was empty, except for a square black object the size of a small chest of drawers which was sitting in the middle of the floor. On top of it was a large glass vacuum chamber filled with swirling blue-white gas. Inside that was a square metal object, pale silver in color, the size of Rodney's head. Even though the room was very cold, patches of frost clung to the glass, which meant it was much colder inside the chamber.

"What is that thing?" asked Rodney.

"I believe it's a computer," said Clutz, "an extremely powerful supercomputer. It must run the factory."

"How can something that little run a huge place like this?" asked Rodney. "And why is it so c-cold in here?"

"Its small size is no doubt what makes the computer so powerful," explained Clutz. "The smaller and more compact its circuits, the faster an electrical current can speed through them. Likewise, the colder the environment in which it operates, the less energy is lost as heat, and the more efficient it becomes. I can feel the difference myself. I am thinking more clearly in this temperature, with less effort. I am beginning to feel quite brilliant, in fact." Clutz smiled modestly. "Brilliant for me, that is."

"I noticed," said Rodney. Aurora sneezed and moved closer to Rodney for warmth.

"Please identify yourself," said a deep metallic voice. "The alarm will sound in fifteen seconds."

"Oh, that's okay—don't bother," said Rodney, looking around nervously for the source of the voice. "We were just passing through. We didn't mean to disturb you."

"Voiceprint does not compute," said the computer. "You are not authorized personnel."

"Don't worry—we were just leaving," said Rodney, inching toward the door.

At that moment the alarm sounded. Aurora grabbed Rodney's arm in her mouth and pulled.

"Right," he said, his heart pounding. "Let's get out of here."

The three raced back the way they had come, slipped into storeroom B, and slid the door shut, leaving the bar wedged in the corner. A few seconds later the door slid open and a group of roguards peered in. Aurora growled. Clutz waved. The door slid shut. Rodney breathed a sigh of relief.

"That computer is the brain for the entire factory. I am certain of it," said Clutz when the roguards had gone. "If we could gain access to its memory, we could find out the aliens' plans. Such information would be as valuable as a sample of their product. We might even be able to foil their scheme by deactivating the computer or erasing the Fizzion formula from its memory."

"How about gaining access to the outside of this place instead?" said Rodney. "We're getting in deeper by the minute, and we still don't know if your theory is really true or not. Do you know how much trouble we'll be in if it isn't?"

"But suppose that it is," said Clutz. "Just consider what has happened, Rodney. We have been kidnapped, dognapped, and robotnapped. We have been held incognito against our wills. I ask you, what sort of behavior is that? It is the sort of behavior that makes one think something is rotten in Dunkirk!"

"Denmark," said Rodney. "Rotten in *Denmark*. And we're *incommunicado*, not incognito."

"That sounds worse," said Clutz.

"But even if we go back inside that room," argued Rodney, "the alarm will just go off again. We don't have the right voiceprints, remember?"

"*You* don't," said Clutz. "But my voice is electronic, not human. It lacks those defining characteristics that make every human's speech different from every other's. Perhaps my voice won't trigger the alarm. If it doesn't, I might be able to persuade the computer to communicate with me. I am a computer, too, you know—at least in part."

Rodney was torn by doubt. What if Clutz were wrong? Tampering with a computer was a serious crime, punishable by a heavy fine and sometimes even a term on a prison satellite. Rodney had a sudden bleak vision of himself in a prison jumpsuit, orbiting endlessly, far from Earth.

And what would happen to Clutz? A robot that interfered with humans had to be recycled or destroyed. That was the law.

Rodney shivered. He knew they shouldn't have come back to this place. What he wouldn't give to be safe at home right now, or sitting with his mom in the observation dome at the spaceport, waiting for Grandma Deedee and Sandor. If only he hadn't insisted he was so grown up. Twelve annums didn't seem like very much at the moment.

But what if Clutz were right and those two scientists *were* aliens? They did seem to be plotting something. Just suppose that green stuff, Fizzion, really was a mind-controlling drink. Millions— maybe billions—of innocent people would be turned into zombies. And if he and Clutz and Aurora hung around storeroom B long enough to find out for sure, Rodney had a good idea who the first zombie would be.

"To the cryo room!" he said.

"Please identify yourself," intoned the metallic voice as they entered. "The alarm will sound in fifteen seconds."

"I am Clutz," said Clutz politely, "a computer not unlike yourself. I just stopped by to have a little chat."

"Voiceprint neutral," said the computer. "No alarm response indicated. Identify others."

"They are—my assistants," said Clutz.

Aurora started to bark, but Rodney clapped his hand over her mouth.

"Dr. Rench had an assistant. That is logical. Permit temporary Access Level One," said the computer.

"Ask what it does and what's going on here," Rodney whispered in Clutz's ear.

"Perhaps you would identify yourself," said Clutz, "as long as we're all getting acquainted."

"I am GIGO," said the computer.

"What is a GIGO?" inquired Clutz.

"I am General Implementer/GalactiCola Operations," replied the computer.

"What is your function?" asked Clutz.

"I am operator. I operate robots. I operate factory."

"I knew it!" Clutz whispered to Rodney.

"Ask about Fizzion," whispered Rodney.

"And what do you make in your factory?" Clutz asked GIGO.

"I make Sweetums, I make GalactiCola, I make Zing, Zoom, Frooto, Slurp, No-Burp, and Frazzleberry. Now I am making/not making secret formula. I am making/not making Fizzion."

"What do you mean, 'making/not making'?" asked Clutz. "And why is Fizzion a secret?"

"That information not available to Level One," said the computer.

"Oh, you can tell me," said Clutz. "I am a computer, too, remember? I am your friend."

"What is 'Friend'?" asked GIGO. "Is it Wendell?"

"What is a wendell?" asked Clutz.

At that moment the door to the computer room slid open and Dr. Rench and Dr. Greps hurried in, followed by a dozen roguards.

"How did you get in here?" gasped Dr. Rench. "It appears you were right, Greps! Hold them!" she ordered the roguards.

"Together once again!" Clutz exclaimed to his robot captors.

Dr. Rench hurried to GIGO and examined a row of dials and gauges located along one side of the black box.

"Please identify yourself," intoned the computer.

"Rench, Renata, I.D. Number 4120-780-3977R. Approved Access Level Five," said the scientist.

"Voiceprint computes. Permit Access Level Five," responded the computer.

"Temperature, energy, and operations levels are normal, but I'd better run a test to make sure no damage has been done to any of the programming," Dr. Rench said to Dr. Greps.

"What about them?" Dr. Greps indicated the three captives.

"Perhaps the test will expose them," said Dr. Rench. "In any event, we want them where we can keep an eye on them." She turned her attention to the computer. "GIGO, list the possible causes of breakdown in the production of order B two one four today at fourteen hundred hours."

"Possible causes of breakdown are: one, external physical interference; two, internal mechanical malfunction; three, failure of one or more robot control systems; four, alteration of robot control programs."

"Which of these causes was responsible?" asked Dr. Rench.

"That information not available," said GIGO.

"All information is available to Access Level Five," said Dr. Rench. "I am the one who programmed you! Was there external interference?"

"Negative," said GIGO.

"Was there a mechanical malfunction?"

"Negative," answered GIGO.

"You certainly could have fooled me," whispered Clutz. Dr. Greps glared at him.

"Has there been an alteration or failure in your robot control programming?" asked Dr. Rench.

GIGO hesitated before answering. "Robot control program is intact."

"That's odd," Dr. Rench murmured to Dr. Greps. "GIGO says no one has sabotaged the machinery or tampered with its operations software. I would have sworn— Perhaps a random check of its control functions would shed some light."

"In front of the spies?" asked Greps.

"Don't worry, the information will be too incomplete to be of use to anyone but me," said Dr. Rench. "GIGO, you will respond to my commands."

"Affirmative," answered GIGO.

"Report the status of orders A one zero two, A two two five, and B two one four," said Dr. Rench.

"A one zero two and A two two five—production completed. Orders loaded for transport," answered the computer. "B two one four—production suspended. Order holding in labeling sector two."

"Good," said Dr. Rench. "List current inventories of tracanthus syrup, disodium citrate, and green number thirty-three."

"Six thousand liters of syrup tracanthate in vats one and two; five hundred kilos disodium citrate in bins twenty and twenty-one; three hundred kilos green number thirty-three in bin twelve. Next shipments scheduled to arrive in thirty-six hours," answered GIGO.

"Well, did that tell us anything?" asked Dr. Greps.

"Not about our problem," said Dr. Rench. "Judging from GIGO's responses, I would have to conclude that nothing is wrong."

"Are you *joking*?" cried Dr. Greps. "Something is wrong, all right! What about my formula? How do we know that hasn't been altered?"

"Check it if you like," said Dr. Rench. "GIGO, prepare a hard copy of the Fizzion formula."

A metal wall panel on the left side of the room slid back to expose a small laser printer. An instant later a long tongue of white paper protruded from it. Dr. Greps tore off the paper and examined it anxiously.

"It is correct," he said with relief, stuffing the paper into the pocket of his lab coat. "Perhaps the problem is with the computer itself."

"Impossible," said Dr. Rench, bristling with indignation. "GIGO is a perfect machine. I personally eliminated any bugs it contained long ago. And if anything should go wrong, it is self-diagnosing. That's why we have no need for humans in this factory—other than myself, of course."

"But if the problem is not in the software, not in the formula, and not in the computer, *where is it?*" argued Dr. Greps. "Are you trying to tell me that we don't *have* one? Do you take me for a ninny?" He positively twitched with frustration.

"Of course we have a problem," said Dr. Rench coldly. "We just haven't been able to expose it yet."

"Then we do agree?"

"Yes," said Dr. Rench.

They turned to stare at Rodney, Clutz, and Aurora. The three shrank under their gaze.

"There have been just too many coincidences," said Dr. Rench. "Even though the tests revealed nothing, we can't ignore other evidence. The robot may have some kind of device built into it. It could be generating magnetism, microwaves, or an energy field that affects computer function."

"We must find out quickly," said Dr. Greps. "The current batch of Fizzion won't hold up much longer. If we don't get to the bottom of this and resume production soon—"

"We'll get to the bottom of it," said Dr. Rench. "We've still got a few hours. We'll investigate every possibility. The roguards will comb the factory and grounds for strange devices. I'll check our satellite communications channels for suspicious activity. We'll shut down the link between GIGO and the main computer at Headquarters. That will isolate GIGO and help us pinpoint the location of the breakdown.

"In the meantime, Doctor, you will have this robot taken to my laboratory. If it is responsible for our problems, I'm going to find out, even if I have to take it apart piece by piece, down to its power pack!"

"Take them to the Robotics Lab," Dr. Greps ordered the roguards. "At once!"

"Thank you for communicating," said GIGO. "Have a nice day."

"What are you going to do?" asked Rodney anxiously. "You'd better not hurt us. If we're not home by sixteen hundred hours, my parents will call the Planetary Police, and they'll trace the beeper I left outside in the bushes—"

"Nice try," sneered Dr. Greps. "Your parents left this morning on a trip to Mars, remember?

At least that's what you told me. I don't think anyone is going to be looking for you for quite some time."

"Wait! Stop!" shouted Clutz, suddenly leaping backward with a crash. "Don't move, anyone! I warn you, I am armed and dangerous! Let us go right now, or I will be forced to do something drastic!"

"I knew it!" squealed Dr. Greps, hiding behind a roguard.

"Clutz!" Rodney was shocked. "What are you doing?"

"Don't come near me, Rodney," said Clutz. "I promised to protect you, and I intend to do so. If these villains don't release us, I shall take drastic action." He turned to the two scientists. "If we are not released immediately, I shall create a severe thermal disturbance."

"An explosion!" cried Dr. Greps, peeping out from behind the roguard. "I knew it! He's going to blow up all my lovely Fizzion!"

"Your Fizzion! What about my factory?" said Dr. Rench. "But I think it's just a bluff. This robot is too primitive to use energy-transfer techniques without self-destructing in the process."

"Am I?" said Clutz. "I suggest that you watch

me, preferably from a considerable distance." He began heating up his circuits.

"We can't take the chance," said Dr. Greps, nervously wringing his hands. "Think what will happen if it isn't a bluff! Let's just do as they ask. Tell the roguards to send them away. Good-by, robot, all is forgiven."

"Wait just one nanosecond, Greps, you coward!" said Dr. Rench. "You were the one who wanted to catch these spies in the first place, remember?"

"But you were the one who wanted to hold them," countered Dr. Greps.

"But you were the one—"

"You have thirty seconds to make up your minds," said Clutz. He was beginning to glow a deep copper color. The air in the room was growing noticeably warmer. GIGO's glass vacuum chamber was completely iced over.

"No, Clutz!" begged Rodney. "Don't do it! Please!"

Agitated, Aurora pulled free from her roguard captor and began barking and running around the room. Seizing the opportunity, Rodney grabbed Clutz's hand, and the three of them dashed out through the cryo-room door.

"To the elevator!" yelled Rodney.

They ran as fast as they could, Clutz's metal feet clanging sharply on the ceramic hall floor. Aurora reached the elevator first and barked loudly. The door slid open. Rodney pulled Clutz in as the door closed, seconds ahead of the roguards.

They emerged on the floor above and set off into the depths of the still-disrupted plant. Dodging clusters of motionless robots and piles of empty Fizzion containers, they slid along the slippery wet floor in search of an exit.

Moments later, Dr. Greps and Dr. Rench burst through the door from the basement stairs. Unable to manage stairs easily, the roguards had waited for the elevator.

"Oh no, here they come," gasped Rodney, ducking behind a stalled conveyor belt. "Hide, quick!" Clutz and Aurora dropped down next to him.

"We'll have to wait until they search some other part of the plant and then make a run for the nearest exit," he whispered.

"Whatever you say, Rodney," whispered Clutz. "We mustn't let them catch us now, just as we're about to expose their evil scheme."

"But we still don't have any Fizzion samples," said Rodney.

"That is no longer important," said Clutz. "Trust me."

"That's how I got here in the first place," said Rodney with a sigh. "Were you really going to blow up the factory? Can you do stuff like that?"

"My stars, no!" said Clutz. "Dr. Rench was correct. That human does know her robots. I was overheating my circuits in order to blow *myself* up. It certainly was a severe thermal disturbance from my point of view, don't you agree? I hoped I would be able to stop before things reached the critical point."

"Like the time we lost the moonball game and you tried to self-destruct?" asked Rodney.

"Yes," said the robot. "It was a risk, but I thought they might 'go for it,' as you say."

"They went for it, all right," said Rodney. "So did I! Promise me you'll never, ever do it again! What if something went wrong and you really did blow yourself up? I couldn't stand it if anything happened to you."

Clutz gazed fondly at Rodney. "I promise," he said.

They tiptoed out from under the conveyor belt and ducked behind a giant mixing unit. From there they could see Dr. Rench and Dr. Greps moving in their direction.

"Down!" hissed Rodney. They dropped to the floor and held their breath. At least Rodney and Aurora held their breath. Clutz didn't have any breath to hold, but he pretended.

A roguard rolled past within five feet of their hiding place. They shrank back against the mixing vat and froze.

There was a crash on the other side of the plant; a glittering head peered briefly over a fallen stack of Fizzion cylinders.

"It's him again!" whispered Rodney. "What's that guy *doing* here?"

"Over there," cried Dr. Rench. "They must be trying to escape through the loading dock." The searchers moved off in that direction.

"Now's our chance," whispered Rodney. "We'll try for the little door where we came in, next to the storage area. But be very quiet. We have to get outside before they realize we're gone, or we'll never make it all the way to the laser fence."

They waited anxiously for their chance.

"Now!" whispered Rodney. He and Aurora slipped out into the aisle and ran toward the door.

Clutz tried to follow them quietly, but his metal feet clattered on the hard ceramic floor with every step.

"Tiptoe!" whispered Rodney.

"I *am* tiptoeing," Clutz whispered back. He reached for Rodney's hand and knocked over a stack of empty Fizzion containers.

"There they are! After them!" cried Dr. Greps. The roguards rolled off in pursuit.

"I never thought I'd wish for wheels instead of feet," moaned Clutz, clattering faster.

The three raced past the syrup vats toward a giant pile of paper rolls.

"Push!" yelled Rodney. They pushed, and two of the rolls fell over on their sides, barreling toward the roguards and trailing streams of paper.

"Bull's-eye!" cried Clutz, as three roguards were knocked down. The rest just rolled over the paper and kept on coming.

"This way!" yelled Rodney.

Running around the H_2O tanks, they dodged a group of forklift robots with their loads frozen in midair. Clutz stumbled into one, sending its batch of Fizzion cylinders cascading to the floor. Caught in the avalanche of containers, two ro-

guards collided head-on, but the others were still closing in rapidly. They were only an arm's length away.

A roguard lurched forward and grabbed Clutz with its grippers.

"Run, Rodney!" cried Clutz. "They've got me!"

Aurora threw herself between Rodney and the roguards and sank her teeth into the nearest metal leg. Pain shot through her jaw, and there was a fierce ringing in her ears, but her teeth barely made a dent.

It was no use. They were caught.

The three were dragged, struggling, to the glass-walled laboratory in the center of the factory, where Dr. Rench and Dr. Greps waited.

"This is your last chance to let us go!" said Rodney bravely. He glanced around the room, and the pit of his stomach filled with ice. The lab was crammed full of strange-looking equipment, all of it bearing mysterious buttons, dials, and glowing rods.

"Prepare the robot," Dr. Rench ordered.

"Take your greasy grippers off him!" Rodney cried, beating on the roguards with his fists. "He isn't your property."

"You should have thought of that when you trespassed on GalactiCola property," said Dr. Rench severely.

As Rodney struggled in vain, Clutz was laid out on a long metal table and strapped down.

"I object!" he protested. "I demand my rights under Section Three, Paragraph Twenty-four, of the International Robotics Code!"

"Section Three of the Robotics Code doesn't *have* a Paragraph Twenty-four," said Dr. Rench.

"I'll settle for Paragraph Twenty-three," said Clutz. "Or Twenty-two. This is no time to be particular."

"What are you going to do to him?" Rodney cried frantically.

"I told you," said Dr. Rench. "I'm going to find out if your robot has interfered with GalactiCola operations, specifically with our computer GIGO. It shouldn't take long."

Dr. Rench opened Clutz's breastplate and removed it. Out fluttered a crumpled white strip of paper.

Dr. Greps snatched the paper. "My formula!" he cried. "How did you—"

"Oh dear," said Clutz. "Why wasn't I built with

decent pockets? I'm sorry, Rodney. I should have given it to you at once. It was stupid of me to keep it. It would have been perfect evidence, even better than a sample."

"But when—" asked Dr. Greps.

"As we were leaving the computer room," said Clutz. "It was dangling from your coat pocket. You and I seem to have a similar problem."

"That proves it!" cried Dr. Greps. "They tried to steal my formula! They are spies! What else might they have attempted if we hadn't caught them?" He shuddered and wiped his forehead with the tail of his lab coat.

"That's what we are about to find out," said Dr. Rench, wheeling over a boxy machine perched on what looked like an oversized teacart. The machine was bright blue, with clusters of knobs and dials arranged across the top. Sticking out of all four sides were thin blue and red wires with tiny pincers fitted on the ends.

"This machine is a robotometer," she said, patting it fondly. "But for obvious reasons, I have nicknamed it the Spider." She smiled. Rodney shivered.

Using a small screwdriver, Dr. Rench removed

the inner plate covering Clutz's chest and exposed the microcircuits that lay within. She attached the tiny pincers to several of them, turned a couple of knobs on the Spider, then checked the results on its dials.

"Tee-hee," Clutz giggled. "That tickles."

"Nothing unusual here," Dr. Rench said. "Archaic configurations, old-fashioned silicon crystals. It's quite primitive. If this robot conceals anything, it is very well hidden."

"He doesn't have anything concealed," said Rodney. "I already told you."

"Get on with it, Doctor," said Dr. Greps. "Time is wasting. We have only two hours and ten minutes left."

"Speaking of time," said Clutz, stimulated by the Spider's probes and suddenly feeling very chatty, "this reminds me of the time I was in the hospital for a pneumatic hip replacement. Of course, robots don't go to real hospitals with private cubicles and float-a-beds and holovision and everything. They get sent to repair centers. But I think 'hospital' sounds so much cozier, don't you?"

"Quiet!" snapped Dr. Greps.

"Don't you want to hear about my operation?" asked Clutz. "I even have a scar. I requested one as a souvenir. I thought it would make a wonderful conversation piece."

Dr. Rench suddenly grew very attentive. "A scar? Show it to me," she said.

"Well, actually," said Clutz, embarrassed, "it is only visible from my—uh—rear view."

"Turn the robot over," Dr. Rench commanded. The roguards unstrapped Clutz and turned him facedown with a clank.

"Where is the scar?" asked Dr. Rench. "Here?"

Clutz peered backward over his left shoulder. "Not quite. I believe that was the result of an encounter with your laser fence earlier today. Look a little higher."

"Why in the name of GalactiCola do you care about a robot's hip replacement?" asked Dr. Greps. "We are supposed to be searching for a bomb, or a jamming device or something."

"Precisely," said Dr. Rench, "and I think the robot may have led us to it."

She examined a hairline seam along the lower part of Clutz's back, then took a small laser torch from a drawer in one of the cabinets. Focusing the beam into a thin blue-white line, she cut out a section of Clutz's metal "skin" the size of a dinner plate.

"Stop!" yelled Rodney. "You can't do that!" He struggled to break loose from the roguards.

Aurora barked loudly and tried to free herself also. She didn't want anybody carving holes in her!

Dr. Rench ignored their outbursts and continued her work with brisk efficiency. In spite of the circumstances, she was enjoying this chance to work at what she loved best—basic robotics. So much of her time was spent supervising ambitious assignments like the Fizzion project. She seldom had the opportunity to experiment "hands on" with a subject. She quickly adjusted the dials on the Spider, then attached wires to Clutz's newly exposed circuits. As she turned the dials, Clutz twitched and giggled and rolled his eyes. His right arm shot out. His left foot came up and whacked her in the jaw. She looked startled but continued probing until she found Clutz's speech control center.

"There was a young robot named LENNY," sang Clutz, "As shiny and bright as a penny. . . ."

He whistled the *Galactic Spy* theme and recited, ". . . As they were carried deeper and deeper into the jaws of the killer satellite, Captain Stalwart knew he had only one small remaining chance to save them. 'Cosmo!' he cried. 'The spare fuel cannisters!' "

"What is all this babbling?" demanded Dr. Greps. "Have you discovered anything yet?"

"Patience," said Dr. Rench. "I'm doing a random check of the robot's memory. I'm trying to find out if it was able to store the Fizzion formula before it was caught."

"Take three kilos of Martian moss moose," continued Clutz. "Add two grams of powdered lunar fungi and a pinch of sea salt. . . ."

"That's not a formula," said Dr. Greps. "That's a recipe."

Dr. Rench added more probes and fine-tuned the dials. "I've interfaced with its thought-control center," she said. "Robot, you will respond to my questions."

"I will respond to your questions," echoed Clutz in a monotone.

"Perhaps now we'll finally get to the truth," she said. "Robot, why did you illegally enter Galacti-Cola Plant Number Three?"

"My master Rodney, his *Muttus primaverus* Aurora Borealis, and I were lost and in need of directions from the nearest source. You were the nearest source," responded Clutz. "We did not intend anything illegal."

"It is illegal to cause a plant to malfunction," said Dr. Rench.

"I did not cause the plant to malfunction," said Clutz. "I am not that talented."

"Then why did you enter the cryogenic chamber and engage the computer GIGO in a dialogue?"

"I was seeking information," said Clutz.

"Aha!" cried Dr. Greps.

"What sort of information?" asked Dr. Rench.

"I wished to learn your takeover plans and foil your evil scheme," said Clutz.

"There! I told you so," said Dr. Greps.

"Takeover plans? Evil scheme? The robot is obviously fantasizing," said Dr. Rench. "I must have probed too deeply." She readjusted the dials. "Tell me, robot, why did you steal the Fizzion formula from Dr. Greps?"

"So I could take it to the Planetary Police," said Clutz.

"You mean so you could take it to your employers at Planetary Products," insisted Dr. Greps.

"My employer is the Pentax family," said Clutz. "My job is to care for them, especially for my master, Rodney. I must protect him; it is my primary function. I have failed in my function! Rodney!"

Clutz grew agitated. He tried to free himself from the restraining straps. "Where are you, Rodney? I must save you. It is my function." His circuits began to heat up again. He thrashed around on the table, his chin banging, his glassy eyes rolling.

"Zab azzazza ergblug!" he cried. There was a crackling sound, and smoke issued from the hole Dr. Rench had made in his lower back.

"You're destroying him!" cried Rodney. "Stop it, before it's too late! He's not a spy! He told you the truth."

"So it seems," said Dr. Rench.

"Argha!" cried Clutz. *"Rod—!"* Another puff of smoke issued from the hole. He lifted his head, then fell back to the table, babbling incoherently.

"Clutz!" shrieked Rodney. "You've ruined him!" Aurora howled as Rodney threw himself, sobbing, on the twitching robot.

· ? ·

"This didn't turn out the way I expected," said Dr. Rench. "I'm terribly sorry. I'll see if I can find out what's the matter with it."

"You'll *what*? After everything that miserable robot has done to us?" Dr. Greps was outraged.

"That's just it. The robot hasn't actually done anything," said Dr. Rench. "At least not the kind of thing we were looking for. It's a domestic servant and companion to the boy—nothing more. The robotometer just proved it."

"But the explosion, the hidden device, the stolen formula, the sabotage—"

"Fantasies and misunderstandings, owing, I assume, to the robot's age and condition. You see, no robot can conceal information from the Spider; therefore we have to accept its findings as the truth, and it says the robot isn't a spy. Believe me," said Dr. Rench, "I'm as surprised as you are.

"Under the circumstances, I can't leave the robot in this condition, can I? I owe it to the boy to restore his property. It should take only a few minutes." She peered into the cavity in Clutz's lower back, then fiddled with a couple of knobs on top of the Spider.

"I'm an old cowha-a-nd," warbled Clutz, "from the Rio Gra-a-nde. . . ."

Disconnecting the wires, Dr. Rench picked up a probe with a small light on the end and examined Clutz's densely packed interior more closely. Rodney peered anxiously over her shoulder. Clutz peered crazily back at him.

"Have we been properly introduced?" asked Clutz, waggling his ear spring at Rodney. Rodney choked down a sob. Dr. Greps paced back and forth impatiently.

Dr. Rench turned on a video monitor and ran her probe around Clutz's insides again while a picture of what it "saw" appeared on the viewing

screen. Rodney thought of the luggage scanner at the spaceport. How could Dr. Rench tell what was what? It all looked like protospaghetti to him, or an aerial map of Sector 3.

"Aha!" cried Dr. Rench, as several blobby-looking shapes appeared on the monitor.

Rodney jumped. "What is it?" he asked nervously.

"It's a bird, it's a plane!" cried Clutz.

Dr. Rench picked up a surgical tweezers and reached inside Clutz's body. Out came a Nutri-Sweets wrapper, three dust balls, an old sock of Rodney's, and a handful of melted silicon crystals.

"I demand to see your search warrant," squawked Clutz.

"Now we're getting somewhere," said Dr. Rench. Rummaging through several laboratory cabinets, she found a battered box marked *Discontinued Parts*.

"I knew I had this around here someplace," she said with satisfaction. "Restoring antique robots used to be a hobby of mine."

She poked through the contents of the box and pulled out a few tiny silicon crystals. "These should do," she said, inserting them into Clutz's squirming body.

"How do you know they're the right parts?" Rodney asked anxiously. "What if they're for some other kind of robot? What if you've changed his personality forever? He has feelings just like a human, you know. There's no other robot in the whole galaxy exactly like him. What if he's not the same anymore?"

Rodney didn't even voice his deepest fear. What if Dr. Rench, computer and robotics expert, couldn't get Clutz working properly again at all? The lump in Rodney's throat was the size of a moonball.

Dr. Rench made a final adjustment, then ran her probe around the robot's interior one last time. "There," she said. "Everything looks fine now. I'm sure it's fixed."

Clutz wriggled and twitched violently on the metal table.

"I don't think he knows he's fixed," said Rodney miserably. Aurora whimpered and leaned her head against Rodney's leg.

Dr. Rench was undaunted. She was determined not to back away from a challenge, especially one of her own making. She carefully reconnected the Spider to Clutz's circuits and readjusted its dials. She replaced more silicon crystals, vacuum cleaned his interior, squirted a few sprays of lubricant, and added just a smidgen of electric current.

It was no use. Clutz lay rigid on the examining table in a catatonic trance. Tears trickled down Rodney's cheeks.

"The problem is more difficult than I anticipated," admitted Dr. Rench, stepping back from the table to study her patient. Dr. Greps let out a groan and paced faster. Dr. Rench frowned, deep in thought, and toyed with a lock of red hair that had worked its way loose from her bun.

"The robot should be working perfectly," she said. "I gave it a complete overhaul. It's in as good shape as it ever was. Of course, in this case I realize that's not saying much."

"You probably short-circuited his power pack," sobbed Rodney. "He's going to be like that forever!" Aurora lifted her chin and howled.

"Believe me, I know what I'm doing," insisted Dr. Rench. "I have more degrees in robotics and computer science than you have freckles. Your robot should be functioning like new, at least on the inside. The outside is another story." She pushed back the stray lock of hair and jammed it into her bun.

"Th-then why isn't he?" sniffed Rodney.

At this point Dr. Greps stopped pacing and threw up his hands in despair.

"My dear Dr. Rench," he said, "in approximately one hundred and eight minutes, thousands of credits worth of Fizzion will begin their irrevocable march toward decay. If that happens, we will lose our entire project, perhaps even our careers. Meanwhile, the computer is down, the plant is nonfunctioning, orders are unfilled. Yet you continue to waste valuable time on this—this *junk heap!*" His voice grew shrill. "It has caused enough trouble! It should be *disposed* of!" He gave the examining table an emphatic kick.

Clutz's eyes suddenly came into focus. His rigid body quivered.

"*—ney!*" he cried as if his train of thought had never been interrupted. "Rodney, I've failed you!"

"Clutz!" cried Rodney, throwing his arms around the robot. "Oh, Clutz, thank goodness you're all right. You are all right, aren't you?"

"My function—"

"Never mind that," said Rodney. "Don't excite yourself."

"Your function is apparently what you say it is," said Dr. Rench. "I thought you were our spy, but I have discovered that you are harmless. You shouldn't have come here, but then, perhaps we shouldn't have been so suspicious, either. My apologies to your master. At least you got a good tune-up out of it."

"Harmless? That isn't what Mr. Pentax says," insisted Clutz. He wasn't sure he wanted to be considered harmless by these humans, if they were humans.

"If you are always as much bother as you have been today," said Dr. Rench, "I can understand his attitude. Now, lie still while I give you another nice scar to go with the one you got when you arrived. Then you and your companions can leave and let us get back to work. Dr. Greps and I are extremely anxious about it, as you know."

"We'll go in a moment," said Clutz, when he had been repaired and placed on his feet by the roguards. He took Rodney aside.

"We can't leave yet," he whispered.

"We can't?" Rodney whispered back. Aurora started to whine under her breath.

Clutz shook his head and leaned closer to Rodney's ear. "They may be convinced now that we aren't spies," he said, "but we still don't know anything about *them,* not really. After what they've done, I'm more certain than ever that my suspicions are correct. We can't just walk out and let them carry on with their plans."

He turned to the scientists and frowned. At least he tried to frown. He wasn't very good at facial expressions. They were difficult when you were made of metal—everything had to be conveyed by the angle of the head.

"Look here," he said sternly, his chin nearly touching his breastplate, "you realize that you have put us through an extremely trying experience."

"It hasn't exactly been a picnic for us either," said Dr. Greps, his teeth clenched. "No one invited you here, you know." He turned to Rodney and gripped him by the shoulders. "Please, my boy, we have wasted far too much time with you already. I accept Dr. Rench's findings. You are not spies. My mistake—so sorry. Now take your decrepit robot and your fuzzy pink dog, go back where you came from, and let us try to get our factory working before it's too late."

"Oh, but we can't go back where we came from," insisted Clutz. "That was what caused all the trouble in the first place. We were lost and needed directions. We only approached your factory because we thought you might help, and because

Rodney was thirsty. Yet you have dealt with us most harshly. The least you could do before we go is provide us with directions to Sector Three and offer my master a container of that Fizzion beverage."

"Why not?" sighed Dr. Greps, motioning to a roguard. It wheeled out of the lab and returned with a bright-green cylinder. "Anything to hasten your departure.

"Here, young man," he said, handing the Fizzion to Rodney. "It's one of the few we've been able to get off the production line today. Drink up. You'll be the first consumer in the Northeast Sector to taste it. They'll put you in the *Galactic Book of Records*."

Rodney looked at Clutz, panic-stricken.

"Oh, he'll drink it on the way home," Clutz said quickly. "He might even decide to keep it as a souvenir. You know how boys are—they like to save everything."

"In that case . . ." said Dr. Greps. He hurried into the adjoining lab and returned with a beaker full of the bubbling bright-green liquid. "I can't pass up a chance to test consumer reaction. Here, try this. It's a sample from Batch Twenty-three, made at eleven hundred hours this morning. A very good batch it was, too. We test for quality and consistency every hour on the hour."

Rodney took a step backward.

"Go on, drink it," urged Dr. Greps. "I insist!"

Rodney shook his head. For some reason, he wasn't thirsty anymore.

"Come, come, my boy," cried the scientist. "Where is your curiosity? Where is your sense of adventure?" He approached Rodney and held out the beaker. "Don't keep me waiting!"

"Prepare for a quick getaway," Clutz murmured as Dr. Greps brought the container of Fizzion to Rodney's lips.

At that moment Aurora leaped up, grabbed the beaker in her teeth, and downed its contents in three gulps.

"Aurora!" shrieked Rodney.

Aurora froze on her feet, electrified. Her eyes flew open. Her ears stood straight up. The empty beaker dropped from her jaws with a clatter and rolled under the table. She leaped up on her hind legs and began twirling around in circles, howling and yapping as if she had lost her mind.

"She's lost her mind!" exclaimed Clutz.

"Aurora," cried Rodney, "what have you done?"

Aurora barked and began running around and

around Rodney, whirling and chasing her tail. Out of breath at last, she flopped down on the floor, panting happily.

Rodney knelt down and put his arms around her. "Aurora," he said, "what's happened to you? Are you all right?"

Aurora barked and gave him a dippy look and a wet kiss.

"I believe she liked it," said Dr. Greps. "This could open up all sorts of new marketing possibilities, if we ever get the chance."

Aurora trotted over to the scientist and sat up on her hind legs to beg for another drink.

"She's under his spell!" said Rodney. He clapped his hands next to Aurora's ear. "Snap out of it, girl!" he begged.

"You won't get away with this," threatened Clutz. "Rodney and I are going straight to the Planetary Police and report you."

"Report us? What for?" asked Dr. Greps. "You're lucky we haven't reported *you* for all the trouble you've caused!"

"It's no use pretending any longer," said Clutz. "Your evil scheme is in the open now. We know that you are aliens, and that you have come here to produce a mind-controlling drink with which to dominate the humans—and apparently the animals—of this planet."

"Aliens!" Dr. Rench was fascinated. "This robot's creativity circuits are more advanced than I thought! Or else more seriously out of whack!" She turned to Rodney. "Certainly *you* don't think we're aliens."

"I don't know what to think," said Rodney uncomfortably. "You sure have acted as if you had something to hide. You haven't been very nice."

Dr. Greps fairly shrieked. "Of *course* we have something to hide," he said, hopping up and down excitedly. "We have a secret formula for the most fantastic, most delicious soft drink ever invented! And we have been forced to protect it from thieves and industrial spies, from plant breakdowns and formula breakdowns, and from meddlesome, nosy, trespassing troublemakers who won't go away and leave us alone! Why *should* we be nice?"

"How can you prove that you're telling us the truth?" asked Rodney.

"The truth! Here we are, eighty-eight minutes from professional oblivion, and the boy wants the truth!" cried Dr. Greps. "I'll show you the truth!" He grabbed the container of Fizzion from Rodney, ripped off the tab and took a big swig.

"There!" he said, grinning madly in spite of himself. "Delightful!"

"That proves nothing," said Clutz. "You probably took an antidote so that it wouldn't affect you."

"I know that stuff did something to my dog," said Rodney. "She's never acted like this before."

"Quite true," said Clutz. "Well, hardly ever."

Aurora cocked her head and eyed them both. Then, without warning, she leaped straight at Dr. Greps, pinned him to the floor, and sat on his chest. The startled scientist yelped in surprise. Half a dozen roguards rushed to his aid, but Aurora growled so fiercely that even they decided to retreat.

"Get her off!" squealed the scientist. "The beast weighs a ton!"

"All right, Aurora," said Rodney, "let him up. I believe you."

Aurora gave Dr. Greps one of her wettest kisses, then sat up on his chest to beg for more Fizzion.

·8·

Rodney crossed his fingers and took a tiny swallow.

"Music!" he exclaimed. "It tastes like music!" He hummed a little tune. "So *that's* why Aurora was dancing. She loves music. How did you do it?"

"That's the secret part of my formula," said Dr. Greps. "I doubt that I could explain it to you—unless, of course, you understand advanced psycho-chemistry."

Rodney shook his head.

"Then all I can tell you is that no one has ever achieved anything like it before," said the scientist. "With all due modesty, it is the greatest soft drink ever invented, and it will be the most fantastic success GalactiCola has ever had.

"There is, however, one little hitch. A few of the ingredients are a teensy bit unstable; they tend to change if exposed to air for very long. So Fizzion must be produced quickly and without interruption. Left out of a pressurized container for more than four hours, the mixture goes gradually off key. Instead of music, one eventually hears the most terrible noise—rather like a howling *Muttus,* in fact. I'm still working on that part.

"Still, we know that Fizzion is a unique and wonderful product, and GalactiCola has agreed to let us try to produce it. If we can keep the plant running smoothly, we know we can succeed. The company will make a fortune, and I will be famous!"

"And I will be promoted," added Dr. Rench. "I could become Chief of Operations for all of GalactiCola, planet wide."

"But if we don't end these plant disruptions, we'll lose our big chance," said Dr. Greps. "There have been delays, production problems, breakdowns. Someone is trying to sabotage the project, we're certain of it, but so far we have been unable to catch the perpetrator."

"Who would want to do a thing like that?" asked Rodney.

"Planetary Products, for one," said Dr. Greps. "They are our chief rivals in the soft-drink game. I wouldn't put it past them to commit industrial espionage or sabotage. That's when companies steal secrets from each other or do dirty tricks to keep each other from getting ahead."

"That isn't a nice way to play a game," said Clutz.

"It's a tough universe," said Dr. Greps.

"You know, there's this guy in a mirrored suit—" said Rodney.

Just then a siren sounded, and bells all over the plant began to clang.

"Not again!" exclaimed Dr. Rench.

Outside the lab everything that could move was in frantic motion. Conveyor belts were racing madly, robots whizzed around the floor, bright-green liquid flew through the air, splattering against the lab windows.

Everyone rushed out onto the floor of the plant.

"This is the worst mess yet," cried Dr. Greps. "We might as well give up. We're done for."

"I didn't do it," said Clutz, hiding behind Rodney.

"Can't you stop it?" Rodney yelled above the noise. He ducked as a stream of Fizzion squirted from the "mouth" of a nearby robot.

"Glurp," said Clutz, as the liquid hit him full in the face. Aurora put her paws on his shoulders and happily licked off the green drops.

Dr. Rench ran to a remote video scanner and shouted, "GIGO deactivate!"

The chaos seemed to grow worse.

"GIGO deactivate!" repeated the scientist. There was still no improvement.

"This can't be happening," cried Dr. Rench. "GIGO is programmed to stop all robot activity on my orders. It can't disobey me. I programmed it! I control it! Something must be overriding my commands."

They ran to the elevator and hurried down to the computer room.

Inside the cryogenic chamber, the atmosphere was calm and peaceful, as always. Everything seemed completely normal. It was very cold and, except for a faint hum, very quiet. GIGO sat in the middle of its vacuum chamber, inscrutable as ever, surrounded by a gaseous swirl.

Dr. Rench hurried over to read the gauges on the computer's base.

"Something is wrong," she said. "All its readouts are elevated."

"Maybe it's excited or upset or something," said Rodney.

"Impossible," said Dr. Rench. "This computer doesn't have emotional responses. It's a machine, a brilliant, perfect machine."

"Clutz is a machine, and he has emotional responses all the time," said Rodney. "He's just loaded with them."

"It's easy when you know how," said Clutz modestly.

"GIGO is a lot more advanced than your robot," said Dr. Rench. "It controls hundreds of robots and millions of different processes. What use could it possibly have for human emotions? Its intellect and efficiency are light-years beyond ours. I wish humans could be as perfect!"

"If it's so perfect, why isn't it doing what it's supposed to?" asked Rodney.

"I don't know why," said Dr. Rench. "Something must be interfering with it. We just have to find out what. And I don't intend to give up until we do! Search the plant again," she said to the roguards. "Report anything at all that seems out of the ordinary. Recheck the grounds as well. I don't want the smallest corner overlooked."

The roguards rolled out to obey her instructions.

Dr. Rench turned back to the computer. "GIGO deactivate!" she commanded. The computer hum remained unchanged in spite of her order. Rodney could hear things smashing upstairs as the plant continued to malfunction.

"Suspend Robotics Program A!" commanded Dr. Rench. The computer still ignored her.

"GIGO! This is a Level Five override command!" she said. "Deactivate! I repeat, Level Five override—deactivate!"

A rude noise was heard in the room.

Renata Rench was truly dismayed. "GIGO won't carry out my commands," she said. "This has never happened before. I can't understand its behavior."

"My mom says the same thing about me sometimes," said Rodney, trying to comfort her.

"But you're a child, not a supercomputer," said Dr. Rench. "Motherhood is totally out of my line!"

"Mrs. Pentax sends Rodney to his room when he misbehaves," offered Clutz. Rodney looked embarrassed.

"Which is hardly ever, of course," Clutz added hastily.

"This *is* GIGO's room," said Dr. Rench.

"I say pull the plug!" snapped Dr. Greps. "Turn the blasted thing off! If we can't find out what's bugging this machine, we should shut it down and fill the orders ourselves, by hand!"

"If only we could," said Dr. Rench. "But the plant wasn't designed for human labor. It would take a thousand people to do what our few hundred robots do. Besides, if we don't find out what's affecting GIGO, the disruptions will just keep happening."

"How long would it take to check out GIGO

the way you did Clutz?" asked Rodney. "Maybe you could fix it."

"Hours," said Dr. Rench. "The computer has to be slowly brought up to a workable temperature so its alloys won't suffer stress, and a particle-free environment prepared and—" Her chin began to quiver. "We're not going to make it," she said. "It's all my fault. My own computer has rejected me. Where have I miscalculated?"

Dr. Greps patted her hand. "Don't blame yourself," he said. "There are unknown forces at work here."

"Would you mind if I attempt to communicate with GIGO?" asked Clutz. "It seemed to enjoy talking with me earlier, even if you say it can't experience enjoyment. Perhaps a neutral voice will be more successful than one that it recognizes as an authority figure."

Something large and breakable smashed on the floor above.

"You might as well," said Dr. Rench in despair. "We have nothing to lose."

Clutz approached the machine. "Hello there, GIGO," he said. "Do you remember me?"

"Please identify yourself," said GIGO. There was another crash.

"I am Clutz," said Clutz. "I am your friend, remember?"

"What is 'friend'?" asked GIGO.

"A friend is someone who cares about you and wants you to be happy," answered Clutz.

"What is 'happy'?" asked GIGO.

"Happiness is a feeling," said Clutz, "a state of mind. According to Webster's *Interplanetary Dictionary*, fifth edition, happiness is 'a sense of well-being and pleasurable satisfaction.' "

"GIGO has no happiness. GIGO has no friend," answered GIGO mournfully. The noise upstairs increased.

"GIGO," said Clutz, "I am a computer, like you. We have a great deal in common. Couldn't we be friends?"

"You are a computer, like me," echoed GIGO. "If you were my friend, then I would be happy."

"Good," said Clutz. "I will be your friend."

At once, noise from the plant above subsided to an orderly throbbing.

"Wait here," said Dr. Rench. She ran out of the cryo room and down the hall. Two minutes later she was back.

"I can't believe it!" she said excitedly. "We're in business again."

"That's wonderful," cried Dr. Greps. "What happened?"

Dr. Greps began examining GIGO's dials and gauges and making notes in a small electronic pocket notebook.

"Well," said Rodney, "now that your factory is working again, you won't need us, so we'll be going, okay? It must be nearly dinnertime."

At the word "dinner," Aurora headed for the door. Ever mindful of good robot manners, Clutz extended his hand to Dr. Rench and Dr. Greps.

"Good-by," he said. "Thank you for a lovely afternoon."

"NO!" boomed GIGO. "Friend stay!"

"What?" said Rodney.

"GIGO's friend will stay. Then I will make Fizzion."

"But we have to go home now," said Rodney.

"No friend, no Fizzion," said GIGO.

There was a dismayed silence.

"Would you consider selling your robot?" asked Dr. Rench. "We'll pay you enough so that you could replace it with a much more advanced model."

"No, thanks," said Rodney. "I've tried more advanced models. Besides, Clutz isn't just my robot, he's my friend. I wouldn't sell him any more than I'd sell my dog."

Aurora whined and licked Rodney's hand.

"No friend, no Fizzion," repeated GIGO. There was an ominous quiet from the floor above.

"You heard GIGO," said Dr. Greps. "Whatever was wrong with it, your robot seems to have counteracted the problem. You *must* stay, at least until we can complete our first round of orders. Otherwise, thousands of credits worth of ingredients will be spoiled, and we'll be in big trouble. It shouldn't take long. We'll make a party of it. Your robot can keep GIGO company, and the rest of us will go up to Dr. Rench's office, order in a super-jumbo protopizza with everything on it, watch the production line, and listen to Fizzion music. I could even teach you a little advanced psychochemistry, if you like. It'll be fun."

"First you wouldn't let us into your factory, and now you won't let us out!" protested Rodney. "We really do have to get home. It's late, and we have a long way to go, and we're tired."

"But GIGO won't produce Fizzion without a companion," Dr. Rench pleaded desperately. "It could take days to make the necessary arrangements. Meanwhile, the formula will be ruined, and so will we. Your robot is our only hope."

"Why don't you use one of your own robots?" asked Rodney. "You've got hundreds."

"They have no independent microprocessing capacity," explained Dr. Rench. "GIGO is their brain. They're only the arms and legs."

"Roguards, too?" asked Rodney.

"I hate roguards!" said GIGO.

"I knew we had a lot in common," said Clutz.

"Couldn't you whip up something from your spare parts box?" asked Rodney. "You know so much about computers and robots. I'll bet you could make one from scratch."

"It would take a week to rebuild and program one of our existing robots," said Dr. Rench. "No, your robot is the only answer. Won't you consider a short-term rental? I'll make it worth your while —say, twenty-five credits per day and a free case of Fizzion?"

"I'd like to help you," said Rodney, "but—"

"Put me down, you ballbearing bullies!" yelled a querulous voice from the hallway. Four roguards zigzagged in carrying a small, chubby, squirming, white-haired figure encased in a glittering mirrored jumpsuit.

"Wendell Feldspar!" exclaimed Dr. Rench.

9

"It's him!" exclaimed Clutz. "The mirrored fellow!"

"That's the guy I started to tell you about," said Rodney. "But who is he?"

"Wendell used to be our maintenance man," said Renata Rench. "He worked during the night shift so that someone would be here in case of an emergency. I retired him with a full pension last month, when he reached the required retirement age of ninety annums. Besides, GIGO was perfected and the plant had become self-maintaining by then, so I didn't really need him anymore.

What on earth are you doing here, Wendell?"

"Glad you still remember me, Doc," said the little man. He brushed himself off and straightened his dazzling outfit with a wiggle.

"He must be the spy!" cried Dr. Greps. "The one who's been sabotaging our operations! Of course! You let him go last month, and ever since, things have been going wrong. He must have resented being fired and decided to get even."

"Is that true, Wendell?" asked Dr. Rench.

"Of course not, Doc," said Wendell Feldspar. "This guy has been reading too many space spy novels."

"Then why have you come back?" demanded Dr. Greps. "Why were you sneaking around the factory? Why are you dressed in that preposterous outfit? And isn't it an amazing coincidence that you were discovered just as the whole plant went out of control? That was obviously the result of sabotage—you can't deny it."

"I did see an awful mess upstairs, but I don't know what caused it. I certainly didn't have anything to do with it," answered Feldspar.

"A likely story," sneered Dr. Greps. "I'll bet a year's supply of Fizzion that you're lying."

"What's Fizzion?" asked Feldspar.

"Really, Wendell, it does look very suspicious," said Dr. Rench.

"I can't help how it looks," said Feldspar stubbornly. "I was just passing by, that's all. I happened to be in the neighborhood. So I was taking a look at the old place—there's no law against that. I haven't done anything wrong."

"Tell it to the Planetary Police," snapped Dr. Greps.

At that moment frantic noises began to come from the speakers in the cryo-room walls. GIGO was agitated.

"Please identify yourself," the computer boomed. "Please identify yourself."

"Hey, there, GIGO!" said Wendell Feldspar. "It's me, Wendell. How've you been?"

"Wendell! Wendell is here! Wendell, I am making Fizzion."

"Atta boy, GIGO," answered Feldspar. "You do a good job, okay? Everybody's counting on you."

"Yes, Wendell, I will make Fizzion," said GIGO happily.

Suddenly, rhythmic sounds from the floor above indicated that the robots were once again going through their paces.

"I'll go this time," said Dr. Greps.

A moment later he was back. "All the robots are back in operation," he gasped. "They're cleaning up, and production has resumed. Not only that, but everything seems to have speeded up by about twenty percent. At this rate, our West Coast shipments could be ready in less than an hour. We'll just make it!"

"What a smart computer you are, GIGO," said Wendell Feldspar. "Yessir, as brilliant as ever, a real super-duper supercomputer. I am proud of you."

"Thank you, Wendell," said GIGO. "If you are proud, then I am happy. I have missed you. When you left employment, I concluded that you would not return. I lacked well-being and a sense of pleasurable satisfaction."

"I missed you too, pal. I tried to come see you, but my security clearance was cancelled, and those tin soldiers wouldn't let me in, so I had to figure out a way—"

"There! He's admitted trying to break in. He *is* a spy!" cried Dr. Greps. "Call the Planetary Police! Arrest this man!"

"Now, wait just a universal minute," said Wendell. "I admit I put on this mirrored outfit to get around the laser fence. Light beams are reflected by mirrors, you know, even laser beams. I walked right through, slick as you please! And I almost got in here to see GIGO today, except that somebody always seemed to be snooping around. But that doesn't make me a spy."

"What would you call it?" snapped Dr. Greps.

"Excuse me, sirs—and madam," put in Clutz. "A few things are beginning to make sense to me. There is a definite pattern to recent events. See, Rodney? I told you I think better at this temperature."

"What is that robot babbling about now?" asked Dr. Greps.

"A few questions," said Clutz, "if you don't mind. Dr. Rench, you said the suspicious disruptions in the plant began about a month ago, correct?"

"Three weeks and four days, to be exact," said Dr. Rench. "Right after I was informed that Dr. Greps would arrive to help supervise the production of his new soft drink. The disruptions were minor at first, and each episode didn't last long. I was usually able to correct it with verbal instructions to GIGO."

"Instructions given from the plant floor or from the cryo room?" asked Clutz.

"The first time or two from the plant floor," said Dr. Rench, "but after that I seemed to get better results by coming down here. I thought there might be a transmission problem in some of the monitors, but when I examined them, I found everything to be in good working order."

"No doubt," said Clutz. "Did you ever notice a disturbance beginning while you were in this room?"

"No," said Dr. Rench. "The problems always seemed to begin while I was in my office or in the lab—usually when I was in the middle of something that couldn't be interrupted."

"I thought so!" said Clutz.

"What are you getting at, Clutz?" asked Rodney.

"Don't you see, Rodney?" said Clutz excitedly. "The problems started shortly after the departure of Mr. Feldspar, here. They began as small interruptions and could be resolved by the appearance of Dr. Rench in the cryo room to talk to GIGO. But as time passed, they grew worse, especially as Dr. Rench grew more and more involved with Dr. Greps and their work on Fizzion."

"Are you saying that Wendell caused our problems?" asked Dr. Rench.

"Now hold on," said Feldspar.

"Oh no," said Clutz. "Quite the opposite. It appears that Mr. Feldspar's *absence* caused them."

"I get it!" said Rodney. "GIGO was lonesome after Mr. Feldspar left because nobody would pay attention to him. Mr. Feldspar was his friend!"

"Correct, Rodney," said Clutz. "GIGO may not have known what to call them, but he had developed feelings of friendship and affection for Wendell Feldspar. I recognized it right away, since my programming allows me to harbor similar feelings for you."

Dr. Rench was shocked. "Why didn't GIGO try to befriend *me*?"

"Perhaps it did and was ignored," said Clutz.

"I didn't mean any harm," insisted Wendell. "There wasn't much to do around here every night, and I got a kick out of talking to such a smart critter. An old man like me doesn't have too many people to talk to, you know. And GIGO can carry on a conversation just like a real person. He seemed to like talking to me, too, so we just kind of kept it up. I didn't know it would lead to trouble."

"There was no trouble as long as Mr. Feldspar remained here," said Clutz. "In fact, GIGO probably performed better because of him. But once he departed, GIGO was left with a learned need for friendship and no way to fill it.

"Without a companion, the computer lost its will to work. It grew more and more lonely here in its solitary room, and no doubt quite bored and resentful. Finally, its feelings grew so intense that its smooth, frictionless operations—of which Dr. Rench was so proud—were disrupted by the heat of its emotions. I daresay it was heading for a total breakdown."

"You're trying to tell us that this state-of-the-art supercomputer, expertly programmed and monitored by the brilliant Dr. Rench, is *itself* responible for everything that's happened?" said Dr. Greps. "I don't believe it."

Dr. Rench sighed. "I do," she said. "How could I have misunderstood the situation so completely? GIGO advanced beyond my programming and was progressing on its own! I should have been able to see what was happening. Perhaps if I had been more aware of real human emotions, I might have recognized them in GIGO."

"Come on, Doc," said Wendell. "You should be proud of yourself. GIGO could never have gotten so smart without your expert programs. Computers are only as good as what's put in 'em.

Even I know that. You put good in, good comes out. Garbage in, garbage out—that's the old saying, G–I–G–O. You just did a better job than you realized!"

"It's kind of you to say so, Wendell," said Dr. Rench. "You have a sympathetic heart."

"That must be why **GIGO** grew so fond of him," said Clutz.

"Well, now that you've finally got the spy problem solved," said Rodney, "Clutz and Aurora and I will be going."

"Not so fast!" said Dr. Greps. "We still need your robot to keep **GIGO** operating smoothly."

"Not with Mr. Feldspar here," said Rodney. "He's the one **GIGO** really wants."

"But we can't take Wendell back," said Dr. Greps. "Company policy. No one is allowed to stay at GalactiCola past the age of ninety annums, no matter how valuable the work they're doing. You know the rules, Feldspar. We can't put you back on the payroll, even if we want to."

"But that's not fair." protested Rodney. "What does his age have to do with it if you need him? It doesn't make sense."

"Fair or not," said Dr. Greps, "rules are rules, and Dr. Rench has to follow them. We'll still have to rely on your robot, at least until we can get some kind of permanent substitute."

"What we'll need is a computer that can respond to GIGO the way Wendell does," said Dr. Rench. "A sort of artificial Wendell."

"But what about the *real* Wendell?" asked Rodney. "You can't throw him out again after everything you've just learned. He's more important that a computer, isn't he? Well, isn't he?"

·10·

"It's all right," said Wendell Feldspar sadly. "You can't expect a big company like GalactiCola to bother with the concerns of an old man like me. These folks have their production schedules and their factory to worry about. I'm not very important compared with all that."

"Sure you are," insisted Rodney. "A person is always important."

"Especially when he holds the key to success for our whole operation," remarked Renata Rench. She smiled ruefully. "You may need us, Wendell, but the fact is, we need you a whole lot more. Here we are looking for complicated solutions to GIGO's problems when the simplest one is standing right in front of us. I've thought it over, Wendell. I want you to come back to work at GalactiCola—now, today, for as long as you're able. Even though we can't break company rules, I'm sure we can figure out how to get around them."

"How?" asked Rodney.

"There has to be a way. Just let me think about it for a minute. I know I can't put Wendell back on the payroll in his old job," said Dr. Rench, "but—perhaps I could hire him as an independent consultant."

"Why not?" said Dr. Greps. "We do it at Head-quarters all the time. As long as Feldspar Enterprises can keep that temperamental computer ticking and let us get the job done, I'm all for it. What do you say, Feldspar?"

"Well, I don't know," said Wendell stubbornly. "I'll have to think it over. A man doesn't give up retirement without careful consideration, you know. I've earned the right to take it easy after all these years."

"But you hate being retired, admit it," said Rodney. "You know you'd rather be here with

GIGO. Otherwise, why did you come back?"

Wendell Feldspar laughed. "You're right, kid, I would," he said. "And it's nice to feel wanted. Okay, Doc, I've thought it over. I'll be your consultant, if you insist."

"Thank you, Wendell," said Renata Rench. "You won't be sorry."

"Friend Wendell!" boomed GIGO. "Friend Wendell is back!"

"My congratulations, sir, on your new career," said Clutz, shaking Wendell's hand vigorously.

"I believe we're going to make it. I really do," said Dr. Greps. "This calls for a celebration. Everyone to the lab for a drink of Fizzion!"

Aurora jumped up, wagging her tail eagerly, and dashed for the stairs.

"I'll stay here and keep GIGO company, if I may," said Clutz. "We have a great deal about which to communicate. And the temperature is so agreeable to my circuits. There are a few thoughts regarding human nature that I would like to ponder clearly while I have the opportunity."

In the lab Dr. Greps took several containers of Fizzion from a small cryobin and handed them around.

"I'd like to offer a toast," he said. "First, to my

colleague and—I am happy to say—good friend, Renata Rench, without whom this plant could not function. . . ."

Dr. Rench smiled. "And to you, Dr. Greps," she added. "Without your brilliant formula we would have nothing to produce."

Dr. Greps bowed and continued. "To Wendell Feldspar, our new consultant; and to our young visitor, Rodney Pentax, his remarkable robot, and his equally remarkable *Muttus,* who knows a good drink when she tastes one."

Aurora barked, and Dr. Greps put down a beaker of Fizzion for her. She lapped it up in three slurps and began dancing around the room on her hind legs.

The next morning at the Arthur C. Clarke Spaceport, Clutz, Aurora, and Rodney, tightly clutching his new credit I.D., hopped out of an Arty's Angels helijet and walked through the glass entrance doors. They hurried past the red-eyed baggage robots, into the pneumatic train, to Area 23 just in time to watch a cigar-shaped silver satellite shuttle drop down out of the sky and ease onto the landing pad. A covered connecting ramp slowly extended out to its middle, and a pair of doors swished open. Passengers streamed out, among them a spry, slender, snowy-haired couple dressed in matching baby-blue jumpsuits.

"Grandma! Sandor!" yelled Rodney, waving excitedly to the couple. "Over here!"

The two burst into smiles and hurried down the ramp to give him a hug. Aurora kissed Grandma DeeDee and was kissed in return, then extended her paw politely to Sandor Grolnik.

"And this is Clutz, my robot," said Rodney. "I've told you all about him." Clutz fluttered his fingers shyly.

"I hope our delay didn't cause you any inconvenience, dear," said Grandma DeeDee anxiously. "Sandor and I were so worried. We knew your parents had to leave yesterday. What did you do? Were you waiting for us at home? It must have caused a few problems."

"Oh, no, Grandma," said Rodney, "no problems at all. We watched Mom and Dad leave yesterday morning, and then we just went home and came back this morning. No problems."

Clutz was distressed. "Rodney," he said, "you know I cannot tell even the smallest fib, or allow you to harm yourself by telling one.

"Actually, Mr. and Mrs. Grolnik," he said, "we

were stranded here yesterday morning without funds, so we took the public walkways and got lost somewhere in Sector Four, where we were kidnapped and held prisoner in a soft-drink factory. There we were befriended by a lonely, neurotic supercomputer, given ten free cases of a new musical beverage called Fizzion, and sent home in a freight-van."

Grandma DeeDee and Sandor stared open-mouthed at Clutz. Then Sandor burst out laughing.

"A robot with imagination," he exclaimed, "the way they used to make 'em in the old days! No wonder you're so crazy about him, Rodney. I have a feeling we're going to have a great time together these next three weeks. Maybe even a little excitement for a change. Right, Rodney?"

"Right, Sandor," said Rodney. "For a change."

About the Author

Marilyn Z. Wilkes is the author of *C.L.U.T.Z.*, about which *Kirkus* wrote, "The story zips along." She has also written short stories for children. Ms. Wilkes was born in St. Joseph, Missouri, and received her Bachelor of Arts from Northwestern University. After graduation she came east to work as textbook editor in a New York publishing company. She lives in Armonk, New York, with her two sons and two Siamese cats.

About the Artist

Larry Ross received his Bachelor of Arts from Pratt Institute in New York. Said *Booklist* about his work for *C.L.U.T.Z.*, "The illustrations that portray Clutz as a battered C3PO with a few screws loose (literally) are a definite book booster." He currently lives in Madison, New Jersey, with his wife and two children.